MEDIAPOLIS PUBLIC LIBRARY
128 N. ORCHARD ST.
MEDIAPOLIS, IA 52637

LIBERTY DOWN

DATE DUE 8/19

Help us Rate this book...
Put your initials on the
Left side and your rating
on the right side.
1 = Didn't care for
2 = It was O.K.
3 = It was <u>great</u>

	DATE DUE		
SEP 1 0 2019			
MAY 0 4 2020			
SEP 0 8 2020			

MRH 1 2 ③
_____ 1 2 3
_____ 1 2 3
_____ 1 2 3
_____ 1 2 3
_____ 1 2 3
_____ 1 2 3
_____ 1 2 3
_____ 1 2 3
_____ 1 2 3
_____ 1 2 3
_____ 1 2 3
_____ 1 2 3
_____ 1 2 3
_____ 1 2 3

PRINTED IN U.S.A.

LIBERTY DOWN

A Corps Justice Novel
Copyright © 2016, 2018 C. G. Cooper. All Rights Reserved
Author: C. G. Cooper
Editors: Andrea Kerr & Cheryl Hopton

GET A FREE COPY OF THE CORPS JUSTICE PREQUEL SHORT STORY, *GOD-SPEED*, JUST FOR SUBSCRIBING AT CG-COOPER.COM

To my faithful readers: thank you for allowing me to continue this awesome writing journey. I could not do this without you.

- CGC

PROLOGUE

Three days had passed since the Republican National Convention ended, and Congressman Antonio "Tony" McKnight was still basking in the glow of public applause. He was now officially the Republican Party's presidential nominee. His opponent was the popular head of state: President Brandon Zimmer, and many believed the Republicans, McKnight specifically, were lagging behind.

In McKnight's opinion, that's where good old-fashioned partisanship came into play. For the most part, people voted along party lines. If they were lifelong Republicans, they'd vote Republican. If they had the slightest liberal streak, they voted Democratic. Sure, there were Independents and the Libertarians, famous for nabbing the occasional headline, but that was a nonissue during this election cycle. Zimmer and McKnight had waged a clean campaign up to this point. When it came down to dissecting their basic beliefs, there were very few differences; they might have almost been mistaken for the same man.

Both were single, good-looking, public servants, who were tough in areas most citizens felt important: foreign policy and immigration. It was no wonder that the two men had become friends and worked closely together on a wide range of policy moves. But now it was election season, and it was time to get serious.

Overall, McKnight arrived at the Republican National Convention (RNC) with a healthy dose of skepticism. As a politician, his skepticism was honed to a needle's point. He left the convention a changed man. It was the human equivalent of taking a normal-sized balloon and increasing its capacity by 300%. With half of the nation behind him, Antonio McKnight was now walking the tightrope of invincibility.

He had been competent most of his adult life, but now, with the full weight and monetary backing of the Republican Party, he was beyond powerful. He was unbeatable.

He left the Convention adorned with the adulation of millions, and while he expected a bevy of new resources, he had been astounded at the variety of gifts offered. He had his pick of the litter; the best of the best clamored for his attention. He couldn't begin to remember the names of all the staffers they had thrown at him. If that wasn't enough, there were the swank accommodations, the motorcades, the round-the-clock security, and every other creature comfort a presidential nominee might desire.

Now, after having time to digest it all, he figured it was time to make some changes, to make some bold moves, and to take the battle to the enemy, so to speak. One outstanding resource had been gifted much like a pretty blue box from Tiffany's. It had been subtle, discreet, yet unmistakably valuable.

Surprisingly, it was the head of the Republican National Committee who had pressed the paper with the handwritten number into McKnight's hand and whispered in his ear, "When you're ready to start digging, call this number."

There was a lot of pressure from his fellow Republicans to pull out all the stops. Up to that point, McKnight had not lifted a finger to attack President Zimmer. However, the gloves came off the moment he placed that phone call.

At precisely 12:15 pm, there was a knock at his penthouse door. McKnight answered the door himself and motioned for the taciturn man to enter. A single raised finger stopped the presidential nominee from speaking. He had been about to offer the man a drink, but instead he watched with curiosity as the man made a pass first through the living room, then the master bedroom and finally through the small kitchen. After completing his inspection, he returned to McKnight. It was then McKnight noticed the earpiece the man wore.

"The Secret Service does make a sweep twice a day," McKnight said, not amused that the man had made his own security evaluation.

"I like to make my own sweeps, Congressman." The man finally held out his hand, and said, "Ian Rourke, sir."

"It's good to meet you, Mr. Rourke. Would you like to take a seat?"

Rourke remained standing. The man unnerved the normally implacable congressman.

"I won't be staying long, sir. I assume you've got an assignment for me."

Now McKnight was confused, although he did his best not to show it. All he had done was place the call; he had not said a thing about an assignment. There was no doubt that the man could be trusted. He wouldn't have been given the name otherwise.

"Why don't you tell me what you do, Mr. Rourke? Our mutual friend was vague on the details."

Rourke nodded, like he had expected as much.

"My firm handles surveillance and counter surveillance.

We rarely take direct action, but when we need to, we can get it done."

"Do you work domestically or internationally?"

"We do both, although overseas much of our work is contracted out. It keeps us in the good graces of the local authorities."

McKnight understood. There was nothing that a foreign power liked less than a bunch of rogue Americans prowling their streets. After all, this wasn't the Cold War.

"And your background? I assume you have previous military experience?"

"No, sir. I was a cop before 9/11, and then I joined the FBI."

"Let me guess—your skill set became more valuable on the outside, so you hung your own shingle and opened for business?"

Rourke nodded.

"I was lucky enough to make great friends in Washington. They keep me busy, and I don't have to look for work."

McKnight wondered who ultimately controlled Ian Rourke. He mulled it over for a moment, and then he pushed the thought aside to consider another day. There were just too many power players in Washington to sift through. By the way Rourke was looking at him, McKnight felt as if he was the one being judged. He felt like a law school grad, plucked out of the employment pool and plopped in front of the senior partner in some shiny New York skyscraper.

He didn't like it, and was about to tell the man to leave, politely of course, when another image came to mind. It was something that had been plaguing him for months. It was still vivid in McKnight's memory, probably because he had been introduced to the memories after what felt like a near-death experience. It was a revelation that had come as a complete shock to him. He had met men like Rourke before, and it was those men who now slipped in and out of the edges of McKnight's nightly dreams, like bat-winged demons waiting for their chance to eviscerate him.

That characterization made him smile; allowing his mind to wander down an entirely new path.

"Mr. Rourke, I just had an idea. I assume your schedule is open?"

"My men and I are at your disposal, Congressman."

"Good." McKnight walked to the window and he looked out over the expanse of Washington, D.C. He could feel the thrumming of energy, ready to burst from the city's seams.

"Have you ever heard of a small group headquartered in Charlottesville, Virginia, called The Jefferson Group?"

"I don't believe I have, Congressman." Rourke didn't take notes. McKnight could see from the man's reflection in the window that the name would not be forgotten.

"I want you to keep an eye on them. Tell me where they go, and tell me who they see. Would around-the-clock surveillance be possible?"

"Yes, sir," Rourke said, without hesitation.

"Perfect. Why don't we start there? How often will you give me your reports?"

"How often would you like them, sir?"

McKnight liked this man. He was cool and efficient, like a python ready to strike.

"Why don't we see how things go for the first couple of days?"

"Is there a particular activity or a certain relationship you would like us to explore?" Rourke asked.

McKnight thought, briefly, about telling Rourke about President Zimmer, and that The Jefferson Group was comprised of men who were not only Zimmer's closest friends, but who might also be a top secret force the president used when needed. McKnight had been lucky enough to be introduced to the men of The Jefferson Group. Zimmer had introduced them as friends, but after spending a full day with them, McKnight could see there was much more than friendship among the men. They were an asset, and the last thing Congressman McKnight needed was his opponent having a potential weapon that McKnight himself couldn't control. That was, unless of course.... Well, there would be plenty of time to think on that.

"Why don't you just stick with surveillance for now, Mr. Rourke? We'll figure out your role along the way."

There were no good-byes or a final handshake. Rourke just gave McKnight a curt nod and left with his marching orders.

It really could all be nothing, McKnight told himself as he once again gazed out over the nation's capital. *But then again...* There was a part of him that had always been more farsighted than his peers. He recognized opportunity. He knew how to grab it, wrestle it to the ground, and choke it until it ultimately yielded to his will. McKnight smiled at the thought.

The search would begin in Charlottesville, but who knew where it would lead? McKnight hoped it would lead to an iron stake in Brandon Zimmer's heart, followed by Congressman Antonio McKnight's golden ticket to the White House.

CHAPTER ONE

"Wow," Cal Stokes said in awe, just loud enough for his girlfriend, Diane Mayer, to hear. He glanced back to get a better view of yet another gilded statue from the top level of the double-decker bus.

Diane squeezed his hand and smiled. They had only been in Paris for two days, and already she had seen a whole new side of Cal. There was this sort of childlike wonder about him as they explored the city. Locals and tourists alike demonstrated deep reverence and respect for the historical meaning and people who had a hand in building modern civilization.

Cal glanced back at her with a questioning look. "Are you laughing at me?" he asked, but he wasn't angry.

"I'm just glad that you like Paris."

"You didn't think I would," Cal smiled, and he was right.

Well, almost right. To call Cal Stokes unworldly was like saying the sky wasn't blue. He had been to too many places to count, and he had seen and done things that only a chosen few would ever experience. Much of that travel had been out of necessity, first as a military dependent following his Marine father across the globe, and then as a Marine himself, fighting

in Iraq and Afghanistan. He'd taken occasional stops in
Europe for R&R, and now there was his current assignment.

While Cal could still, at times, look like a fresh faced,
thirty-year old man, he wasn't that young. He was a brave
warrior and respected among his peers. He was a man who
wouldn't think twice about running into danger to save a
friend's life, even if it put his own at peril.

But while Cal was well traveled, he also held a healthy,
more realistic view, regarding much of the world. He made it
plainly known early on in their relationship that France was
one of the few places he hadn't been and one of the last he
felt he would ever visit. Now here he was, gazing out over
Paris like a man who just regained his sight after years of
struggling blind.

"I'm just happy you like it," Diane said, squeezing his
hand again.

"Let's just say I'm pleasantly surprised."

"Do you think Daniel likes it?" Diane asked.

Daniel Briggs worked for Cal at The Jefferson Group
(TJG), a Charlottesville, Virginia based consultancy. On
paper, TJG helped companies and institutions with everything from technology to security. It was what they did off
the record that made Daniel such a valuable commodity.

Daniel was still an enigma to Diane, and even though she
was in the Navy, and her family came from a long line of law
enforcement, she had instantly recognized that Daniel Briggs
was a cut above, maybe even higher than Cal himself. Not
only was Daniel the tip of the spear, as Cal liked to say, he was
also Cal's constant shadow and his best friend. He was always
there with a quiet word to calm Cal or to provide sage counsel. It had taken Diane a bit to become accustomed to the
vigilant guard's constant presence.

Even now she found it slightly uncomfortable that the

former Marine sniper sat a mere ten rows behind them on the bus.

"You know Snake Eyes," Cal said with a grin. "If there's an opportunity to sit in one place for hours at a time without uttering a word, he'll snatch up that opportunity in a second."

"Honestly, Cal, don't you think he'd be better off spending time on his own? I mean, this is supposed to be his vacation as much as it is yours, correct?"

"Babe, I promise you; he's fine." Cal had explained it to her on more than one occasion: it wasn't just Daniel's job but that he saw it as something like his duty to stay close to Cal. If Cal, who hated anyone looking over his shoulder, could deal with it, then maybe she could too.

Right then and there, Diane resolved to put her unease aside. Daniel was Cal's best friend, and so long as that didn't get in the way of their personal relationship, there shouldn't be anything wrong with having the sniper around. He had saved Cal's life on more than one occasion, after all, and what selfish girlfriend wouldn't want her significant other to be safe, especially in his line of work?

Forty minutes later, when the recording in their earphones announced they were approaching the Moulin Rouge, Cal nudged her. "Hey, why don't we hop off and get a coffee? You think they have any of those chocolate croissants around here?"

Diane rolled her eyes. "There's a patisserie on every corner in Paris, Cal."

But when she turned to face him, she saw a wide grin. He was teasing her.

When the three stepped off the bus, Cal was quick to point out a fancy looking café on the corner, the black awnings in stark contrast to the chrome tables and chairs lining the sidewalk. It was just the kind of place Diane liked to avoid. She did a quick scan of the street and finally found what she was looking for.

"Let's go to that one," she said, pointing in the opposite direction. There was a little mom and pop café with an old faded sign, but the front window was piled high with pastries.

"Are you sure you don't want to get a cup of coffee and sit down? You're the one who likes to people-watch," Cal said.

"She's right, Cal," Daniel said, surprising Diane. "The place she pointed out is better."

"Why do I have a feeling that you have either cased that joint or eaten there before?"

Daniel shrugged, "Why can't it be both?"

Diane looked between the two men, who were now grinning at each other as if they shared some private joke, and made it her mission, while in Paris, to get to know Daniel better. In that moment, she vowed to increase her understanding of the man behind the camouflaged curtain, the one even the toughest warriors trusted with their lives.

Diane stepped between them, grabbed one arm each, and started marching.

"I am about to dazzle you Marines with my impeccable command of the French language."

Pastries and coffees in hand, they meandered in and around the horde of tourists.

"Twenty bucks says I'm ten pounds heavier by the time we fly home," Cal said, digging into his second chocolate croissant. Before Diane could respond, Cal continued, "That reminds me. Have you noticed that there aren't a lot of overweight people here? I mean, is it just me, or do they keep those people hidden?"

"It's due to the food and the exercise," Diane explained. "They have a different attitude about it here. Look around you. People walk everywhere. Sure, they take trains and some people own cars, but even in metropolitan areas like Paris, people are just used to walking."

Cal stopped cold, raised his hands in shock. "Hold on a second. Are you telling me that if we moved to Paris, as long as I kept up a walking regimen, I could eat as many of these as I want?" he asked, pointing to the half-eaten pastry in his hand.

Diane looked at Daniel. "Is he this much of a smart ass at work?"

"Pretty much."

Diane shook her head, then stepped over and grabbed Cal by the front of his shirt. "Smart ass or not, Cal Stokes, I can't imagine you moving to Paris, France, in a million years."

She stood on her toes and kissed him on the lips, but he didn't kiss her back. She thought something was wrong for a moment until he said, "Let me get this straight. You're saying that if we move to Paris, France, and as long as I keep walking, I could keep eating these *and* kiss pretty girls on the street?" He was smiling wide now, quite happy with himself.

Diane was about to drag him down for another kiss, but she felt Cal tense, and she saw him glance at Daniel.

"What is it?" she whispered.

"It's probably nothing," Cal said, dead serious.

Diane heard the commotion and looked back to see two males sprinting out of the crowd, elbowing their way clear. A moment later another man burst forth, chasing them, wearing what looked like a sailor's outfit. Where had she seen that before? Oh, yeah, it was in one of those restaurants where the waiters dress like sailors, wearing white Dixie cup hats and blue smocks.

It looked like there was no way the waiter could catch them. Cal and Daniel must have figured that out too, and Diane figured something out in the split second before it happened. She was traveling with two men of honor whose day job was to fight injustice. However, as if to accentuate their goodness, if a crime went down it was a sure bet they would lend a helping hand.

It looked like the manager of the restaurant, with a bulging belly and huffing cheeks, was now running after the other three men.

"Stay here," Cal said to Diane. Before she could answer, Cal and Daniel were off, dropping their pastries to the ground as they gave chase. All she could do was stand in place and watch as they sprinted out of sight.

* * *

CAL WAS SURPRISED as Daniel flew by him while Cal grunted as he hurdled the short fence next to the bus stop.

"I'll get the one on the left," Cal said.

They had already passed the waiter, yelling his encouragement, in French, to the two Americans. It was a good old-fashioned foot race. Neither Cal nor Daniel were armed.

Cal wondered if they were doing the right thing. It had been pure instinct that had pulled them down this path. They were supposed to be on vacation. For all he knew, the two guys up ahead were just petty thieves, not worthy of their time. He pushed that doubt aside as a car blared its horn and swerved to miss him. Cal was fast, but Daniel was faster. He was already a couple strides ahead, laser focused on his man.

The guys up ahead split, one running to the left and the other to the right. Cal followed his target without hesitation, but now the young man looked back and saw Cal gaining. Without breaking stride, he tipped first, and then another trash can over, hoping to impede Cal's progress.

A long stride carried Cal over both, which actually helped him pick up even more speed. He was mere feet away now. While he didn't want to dive, he could if he had to. Diane might be pissed if he tore the clothes she had just bought him, though. *I can deal with that later.*

Cal was just reaching out to grab the guy by the back of his shirt when the thief did something impossible. Without stopping, he just planted his feet and rocketed 90 degrees to the right, doing a perfect double flip, landing on top of a parked car. The kid actually had the balls to look back at Cal and sneer, like it was all just some teenage prank.

The look fueled Cal's anger and he lunged for the thief. He narrowly missed the guy's pant leg. If Liberty, Cal's just over a year-old German Shorthaired Pointer, had been with him, the game would have been over already. However, she was back at the hotel.

Cal swung around the parked car while his target did another flip onto the street and was once again streaking away.

Cal had enough. There was a homeless guy a few feet away who had stopped to watch the fun with a toothless grin, obviously enjoying the entire spectacle. He had a brown bag in his hand. When Cal looked his way, he saw the unopened can hidden inside. Cal grabbed it without thinking, and with a great heave, he threw the oversized beer can at the running target. His aim was true, and the can crashed into the back of the young man's knee, tumbling into and finally laid out within a group of gawking Asians holding up selfie sticks like they had been waiting for the finale.

Cal was on the kid in a second, pressing him to the ground, face turned. The young man looked shaken but not hurt.

"Don't move," Cal said, pressing his knee into the man's upper back. The guy went limp like he was used to being roughed up. Maybe he'd been arrested a few times. He just laid there, cheek against the pavement, taking in quick breaths.

A few seconds later, the waiter appeared, muttering obscenities at the man under Cal's control. Once he had gotten that out of his system, he looked at Cal and in accented English said, "Thank you, Monsieur, he steals from the restaurant."

He fished in the man's pockets and came out with a handful of Euros. Cal estimated there were probably a couple of hundred dollars in the man's hand. No treasure hoard, but a fair haul for the young punk.

"Shouldn't you call the police?" Cal asked the waiter.

For a moment, the waiter seemed unsure, then he shook his head. "No, no."

He raised the money and pointed to it as if that was all that mattered. Justice had been done. Before Cal could protest, Daniel appeared, pushing the second man, pain registering on the man's face from the arm bar that Daniel had him in. Daniel looked calm as always, like it was the most natural thing in the world to catch a thief on the streets of Paris. The waiter repeated the verbal scolding to thief number two and then fished out more bills from the second culprit's pockets.

A few French obscenities later, the red-faced, out-of-breath manager appeared. When he stopped running, he doubled over, hands on his knees. It took a full minute before he could speak. The waiter asked him something in French, and the manager waved him away.

He said something to Cal, but Cal didn't understand French.

"Oh, American," the manager said between labored breaths. Cal nodded. "Let them go. They will not be back." He turned to the two thieves. "I know your faces," and with that primal warning, Cal and Daniel let the thieves go.

Cal was surprised they didn't run off. They just gave the manager and the waiter not necessarily an apology but more like an acknowledgment. An armistice had been negotiated. Off they went as if nothing had happened.

There was a quick back-and-forth banter between the waiter and the manager. The bills were given to the manager. The debt had been settled, and the waiter trotted off, no doubt to take care of his remaining tables.

The manager looked up at Cal and Daniel. "Are you staying in Paris?"

"Yes," Cal answered.

"May I ask where?"

While normally Cal wouldn't divulge such information, he was in Paris, after all. What could it hurt? Besides, Paris was a big city.

"We're near the Champs-Elysées, a couple of blocks from the Louis Vuitton store," Cal said.

The manager clapped his hands in delight. "Ah, how wonderful! My two brothers have a restaurant not far from there, maybe a block. You will be their guests tonight, say nine o'clock?"

"That's really not necessary," Cal said. "We already have reservations."

"No, no," the manager said emphatically. "They have— how do you say—a tasting menu. You sit and they feed you. I will call them now to tell them you are coming. Just the two of you?"

When in Paris? Cal asked himself. "Actually, there are three," Cal said, glancing at Daniel.

There was a slight hesitation from Daniel.

"Three for nine o'clock, yes?" the manager confirmed.

"Would it be a huge imposition to make it four guests?" Daniel asked.

Now that surprised Cal. The extra guest was news to him, but he didn't question it.

"Yes, yes. Four guests for nine o'clock. And can I have a name, Monsieur?"

"Stokes," Cal answered, throwing Daniel a look.

"Yes, Mr. Stokes. The restaurant is called Philippe et Jean-Pierre at Seven Rue de Boccador. My name is Fabio, and I thank you for your help. Here is my card. You come by the neighborhood; please stop by and see me. We have the best mussels in Paris."

With that, the man was away, the caper solved, and all was right with his world.

Daniel answered Cal's unspoken question before Cal could get it out.

"I was going to tell you guys on the way back to the hotel. I hope you don't mind if a friend joins us for dinner."

It would be the first time Daniel had ever introduced Cal to anyone outside of work. "Sure, of course, no problem. Diane will like that. And what's his name?"

Daniel actually looked confused for a moment, a total split from his normal rock-steady demeanor. "It's a she. She's —well—she's an old friend. I didn't know she was in town until this morning. You're sure Diane will be okay with that?"

Cal smiled and clapped his friend on the back, "Buddy, you have no idea how happy she's going to be."

And with that, the two men retraced their steps to find Diane.

* * *

WHILE NORMALLY CAUTIOUS and always observant of every-thing around them, the sprawling city betrayed them. Neither man noticed the moped on the side street with the single rider on board. The rider's face was obscured by the black helmet. To anyone watching, it looked like the driver was merely looking at his cell phone screen, but as the two

Marines slipped from view, the driver ended the recording and tapped a couple of buttons.

In less than a minute, the entire video had been sent. His duties now complete, the driver revved the small engine and went off to find the two thieves. They had already been paid half their fee and would undoubtedly haggle for more. He would only pay them what they'd first agreed. They would take it. After all, they weren't savages. They were civilized Parisian thieves making their income the only way they'd come to know.

CHAPTER TWO

For the rest of his adult life, Gaucho would remember Amsterdam for two things. First, the smell of marijuana as they walked out of the train station. It wasn't like the city pumped it into the air or anything, but there had been a pair of dreadlocked friends just outside the terminal, lighting up as if it were the most natural thing in the world.

The second thing was bicycles. Outside the Amsterdam train station, there were thousands of bikes parked, locked, and waiting for their owners. When they had taken a cab to their hotel, the driver had said, with obvious disgust, that bikers were the terrorists of Amsterdam.

Gaucho had seen it with his own eyes: bikers seemed to care little for their automobile driving counterparts, zipping across traffic lanes, cutting in front of any vehicle, large or small. When he pressed the driver about it, the man had said that the laws in Amsterdam were clear. No matter the consequences or where the fault truly lay, if you hit a bicycle, it was the vehicle driver's fault.

He had watched the delicate interplay, like a teenage

dance, all unspoken rules and petulant players, as they weaved their way through Amsterdam. Gaucho smiled as still another city surprised the otherwise worldly former Delta operator.

He and his traveling companion, Willy Trent, a near seven-foot tall former Marine Master Sergeant, deposited their luggage at the boutique hotel oddly named JL No 76. Its lobby was decorated with modern zeal. The open bar served guests who would simply fill out a card and pay when finished, several drinks later. It wasn't necessarily the Hispanic's choice of décor, but he did appreciate the quirkiness of it, including the set of four dog statues in the hotel window sporting helmets in bright colors and squatting to do their business.

"Come on," Willie said. "Our Uber driver is almost here, and I'm starving."

Gaucho wondered how his friend could be hungry again. They had taken a first-class cabin on the train from Paris and they had eaten well. Gaucho was still full, but he knew from experience that the NFL linebacker-sized Marine walking next to him needed nearly constant replenishment.

"You know, Top," Gaucho said, using the name reserved for friends of Marine Master Sergeants, "I know we're on vacation and all, but you better watch what you eat. You don't want to go losing those washboard abs."

Willie turned and laughed, and it sounded more like a boulder avalanche than an ordinary man's chuckle.

"I plan on eating my way through Europe...washboard abs be damned."

Gaucho laughed along with his friend. It was absurd for sure. Only a 365-day McDonald's binge could possibly nudge Top's abs into anything but perfect form, and even then, he'd have to ignore any healthy choices.

Their Uber driver arrived, instantly wide-eyed, gawking at

the huge Marine walking up with Gaucho. The driver gave them a leery nod as they entered the car, a BMW sedan that was too small for Top, but he didn't complain. Top never complained.

That was one of the things Gaucho liked about his friend. That might be why they had become best friends. Willy Trent had a way of looking at the world that could probably convince even the most cynical of men that everything was going to be okay, that life was as it should be, even if it wasn't at that moment. The stars would soon align, and everything would be just fine.

"You ever have fondue before?" Top asked over his shoulder.

"I think I went to a Melting Pot once on a date," Gaucho said.

"Well, the place I'm taking you to has some of the best fondue I've ever tasted. I tried to convince the chef once to give me the recipe but he wouldn't budge. He's a stubborn old coot, but I think you'll like the food."

"How many times have you been to Amsterdam?"

The dark green Marine let out a low whistle. "I can't rightly say. I came here for the first time as a Lance Corporal, all bright-eyed and bushy-tailed. Fell in love with the people and the food and I guess, as they say, the rest is history."

"Then lead on, dear leader," Gaucho said. "I am at your disposal."

Ten minutes later, they were dropped off at what the driver said was a diamond museum. He was in fact a fountain of knowledge once he got used to the huge man sitting next to him. He recommended taking the boat tour, as it was the best way to see Amsterdam during the day and at night. The driver said, "Amsterdam is lovely at night with the lights on the bridges."

Top had smiled and nodded along, as if he'd seen and done it many times before. Gaucho could only guess why the city held such affinity for his friend, but he let the thought pass. There would be plenty of time for questions. They were on vacation, after all, a much- needed vacation. Gaucho was with his best friend and they both wanted to enjoy every possible wonderful experience.

The restaurant bar was a leisurely stroll from their drop-off point, and as they walked, Gaucho felt himself fall in line with the flow of the city. Amsterdam seemed to be as much of a tourist capital as Disney World. Europeans and Asians passed by Americans and Middle Easterners. An interesting mix to be sure, but the city felt safe, safer even than Paris had seemed.

When they finally arrived at Cafe Bern, Gaucho was prepared to enjoy the city. He even surprised himself when his stomach grumbled as they walked inside and the smell of food hit his senses.

"Is Lydia in?" Top asked the man at the bar.

"Lydia!" the man yelled to the back.

A few moments later a brunette dressed in jeans and a T-shirt came out. She had large green eyes and the sturdy physique of a woman who wasn't afraid to climb a mountain.

"Willy," she squealed as she ran into Top's arms.

"Girl, you haven't changed a bit." When they finally separated, Top turned to Gaucho and said, "Gaucho, I'd like for you to meet a good friend of mine. This is Lydia. She's taken care of me more times than I can count. Lydia, this is my friend, Gaucho."

"It's a pleasure to meet you," Lydia said.

"You too, Lydia," Gaucho replied and then sniffed the air. "Hey, can you tell me what that smell is? I can't believe I'm saying this, but I'm actually hungry again."

Lydia smiled, displaying a set of pearly white teeth. She was beautiful. Why hadn't Top mentioned her?

"We are just making the sauce, and the bread is almost ready. Would you like a table, Willy?"

Top nodded and Lydia ushered them to a corner table with a good view of the rest of the restaurant. The place looked newly renovated, and when Gaucho asked Lydia about the fresh coat of paint, she confirmed that they'd only reopened a day earlier.

The restaurant wasn't large, but it was dark in the way of the old taverns, and it was perfect for two guys who were used to keeping low profiles. Top ordered for them both, and they started with salads and beer - a local lager Lydia recommended. Top had downed his and asked for another before he had finished his appetizer.

Lydia returned with a second beer for each of them and then began to construct the elaborate wire platform with two sides holding a Bunsen burner under each. She went about her task as if she had done it a thousand times. She explained to Gaucho: the fondue cheese was located on the right side, and on the left side was where they cooked the meat. Gaucho had no idea what she was talking about, but he went along with her explanation.

"Do you remember how to do this, Willy?" Lydia asked. She was obviously attracted to him.

"I could do it in my sleep, honey."

The young woman laughed and returned a couple of minutes later with a basket full of cubed bread, and a platter of sliced meat that looked like filet. She deposited the food on the table, then went to greet a trio of customers just walking through the door.

"So, the way you do it," Top said, picking up a long skewer, like a miniature version of what you might use to cook a marshmallow over a campfire, "is to stab a couple of slices of filet and stick them in the sizzling pan on the left." He ladled a green sauce into the pan as he spoke. "You've got to keep an eye on it to prevent the sauce from burning. While the meat cooks, dig in with the bread and cheese on the other side."

Gaucho watched his friend and then mimicked his movements. "That is good," Gaucho said with a mouthful of bread fondue. He didn't remember liking fondue before. He liked this. When the meat was ready, he savored every bite.

They were almost done with the hearty meal, rarely talking as they stuffed themselves, when Gaucho saw Top's eyes flicker to the door.

"What is it?" Gaucho asked, sipping his third beer coolly. He had his back to the entrance, something he didn't usually do, but these were Top's stomping grounds. It would have seemed odd indeed if they sat alongside one another.

"Probably nothing," Top said, stabbing another cube of bread with his skewer. To anyone else, Willy Trent might have looked completely at ease, but to his good friend, Top was on high alert. Then it was gone like it had never happened. "Yeah. Probably nothing," Top mumbled, taking a sip of his beer.

It was easy in their line of work to get jumpy about every stranger that walked in the door, but when Gaucho pressed his friend about it later, Top just said that there was a tourist who had come in the restaurant asking for directions.

"I was imagining things," he explained, "But I swear he looked right at me and then didn't do it again, even as he was leaving."

The price they paid for being operatives was eternal vigilance. It was easy to see why other men in their line of work rarely relaxed and lived like hermits, but the two companions had seen too much of the evils of the world to let possible problems get them down. Sure, there were bad people out there, and at times they were after the operators from their company, The Jefferson Group. This was a rare occasion — a nonworking vacation - and they both intended to enjoy it.

As they both said their goodbyes to Lydia, Gaucho couldn't help but notice the tingling sensation creeping up his spine, that familiar sixth sense that had kept him alive for so many years.

Relax, Gaucho told himself.

"So, what did you think of the food?" Top asked, as they walked away from the bar.

"Are you asking about the food or about the girl?"

Top was straight faced when he said, "I have no idea what you talking about, Señor. Lydia is a lady and a good friend."

Gaucho snorted, despite his sudden unease, "Don't give me that line. I saw you two looking at each other the whole time. Tell me, what's the deal? Did you guys date?"

Top shook his head sadly, "Alas, our stars never aligned. That's poetic talk for 'she always had a boyfriend'," and then Top grinned, his smile wide, all mischievous and Willy-like. He raised a finger in the air to accentuate his next point. "It turns out she is currently single."

"Hey look, Top, don't let me get in the way. I know we're on vacation and all..."

Top waved the coming offer away. "The lovely Ms. Lydia will be joining us for dinner. It's a place on the water. She said we'd like it. Some new restaurant called The Wolf. They serve fifteen courses over four hours. And, lucky for you, she's bringing a friend."

Gaucho's ears had perked up with that. His life had been too hectic for too long to start, let alone maintain, any kind of relationship.

"Well, aren't you full of surprises?" Gaucho said, patting his friend on the back.

As they walked and chatted through the cobblestone square, while returning to the hotel, Gaucho couldn't help but notice a man in a white track suit staring at them intently. Gaucho marked the face casually and carried on his conversation with his friend.

CHAPTER THREE

Neil Patel stifled yet another yawn on the back of his hand as he scanned his daily reports on his souped-up iPad. The device had the Apple company logo on it, but as usual, he had tinkered with it himself. Now it was fully secure against hacking attempts due to the encryption he had added to the network, but it still ran with the efficiency he liked to call "greased lightning."

"Mr. Layton, could you tell us why you decided to step away from your technology firms to pursue your current path as a consultant?"

Neil looked up at the question, mildly interested. He had traveled to Vienna, Austria, with the CEO of The Jefferson Group, Jonas Layton, a self-made billionaire. Many in the venture capital technology world had given him the moniker "The Fortune Teller." Layton had an almost otherworldly sense for predicting the future of certain markets, and he was often sought out for his counsel and prognosticative powers.

They were in town for a couple of days, serving on a series of panel discussions concerning technology, innovation, and the nuances of international startups.

In his always charismatic tone, Layton replied to the man in the audience. "I won't say that I was bored. I'm rarely bored, but I will say that I was looking for something new, more interesting, and to be quite honest, the role of mentor appealed to me. While you may think being the CEO of a major corporation gives you the daily chance to be a mentor, that is not always the case. There are a lot of other things that many of you have already experienced that go on behind closed doors, and at the time, I was ready to get away from that. The politics and the handholding were my least favorite duties to perform as a CEO. That's not to say that I won't ever go back, but at this moment, I enjoy doing things like this... speaking with new friends like you. I also enjoy helping companies and government agencies sift through the distortions and lay a firm path."

"Might this have anything to do with your relationship with the president, Mr. Layton?" the man in the audience pressed.

Jonas didn't hesitate. Neil was listening intently now. "I am lucky enough to call President Brandon Zimmer a friend. We have collaborated on a handful of dilemmas, and if he called, I would of course drop everything to help. He is a good man, an exceptional leader, and someone who I think the international community can expect big things from in the coming years. Next question," Layton said, pointing to a woman who had had her hand raised in the back of the packed room. The man who had asked the previous two questions interrupted her.

"Mr. Layton, what do you think about President Zimmer's policies concerning America's European allies and his strong stance against Russia and China? Many say that it's a classic case of saber rattling to win over voters prior to your American elections."

Layton smiled as if he knew the question had been

coming. "While I don't normally talk about politics in these sessions," Neil saw the manager of the event just off stage look uncomfortable. This was supposed to be Jonas's show, a glimpse into the daily life of a visionary CEO. "I will say that occasionally a little saber rattling is needed, particularly if you are going up against a twelve-year-old from Tulsa, Oklahoma, who has made it his personal mission in life to destroy you in World of Warcraft."

The audience, a hand-picked selection of business students from the region, all laughed dutifully, but the man who asked the question did not look amused. He opened his mouth to assert himself yet again, but the event manager took center stage and announced, "I'm sure you will all understand that we are running over on time, so maybe one more question from the young lady in the back."

After the session, Jonas had shaken hands with half the kids in the room. He rejoined Neil and their third companion, Dr. Alvin Higgins, a portly, bespectacled man who was wearing his always-present tweed coat. Higgins was as valuable a member of The Jefferson Group as were its CEO, Jonas Layton, and its chief technology officer, Neil Patel.

"I think you handled that quite well," Dr. Higgins said to Jonas.

"I can't say I wasn't expecting it," Jonas said, "but I thought they had screened the audience a little better."

"What can you do? It is an election year," Neil said, "and if there is anything I've learned since getting off the airplane, it's that Europeans are fascinated with our electoral process."

Neil's companions both nodded. All three had been inundated with not-so-discreet questions from students, moderators, and fellow panel leaders. It seemed that all of Europe had turned their eyes on America, and even though this election cycle didn't seem contentious, they were still fascinated. Maybe it had something to do with the movie star-like quality of both candidates, or maybe the Europeans were more aware of the power of American policy over their own bottom line than would be true if the roles were reversed. Either way, Neil knew that many of their cousins to the east would be watching any pertinent news leading up to election night.

Just then, the event manager walked up, his face flushed. "Mr. Layton, how can I ever apologize?"

Jonas put a hand on the man's arm. "It's okay, truly. If I got in trouble for every time I asked a pointed question in college—well—let's just say I'd probably be in federal prison."

The joke went right over the event manager's head. He was clearly perturbed, and no level of soothing would relieve his concerns in the near future.

"But really, Fitz, it's okay. Let them ask their questions. I am happy to answer each and every one, within reason of course."

The man nodded his head, but he was far from convinced. He shuffled off, no doubt to find the young culprit and admonish him for his rudeness.

"What do you say we go upstairs and have some lunch? It's on me fellas. Everything's paid for."

Neil said, "I know."

Jonas chuckled. "I was just being a smart ass. Come on. I'm hungry as hell, and I sure could use a beer."

As Jonas put in the order for room service and Dr. Higgins went to another room in the palatial suite to make a phone call, Neil slipped out his laptop and began clicking away. This was supposed to be a working vacation. Technically, there was supposed to be more of an emphasis on the *vacation* part, but when you were in charge of the data security for one of America's most covert entities, you were never really off duty.

Neil had built the entire system himself, and he knew the ins and outs of his system better than he knew his own body.

So, as he clicked through reports and made his routine checks, his mind sped along as if on autopilot. It was not until he was scanning through the most recent batch of email logs that he paused.

"That's strange," he said to himself. He scrolled down further, then backed up, comparing as he went. It must have been a trick of his eyes. Perhaps it was just the jet lag that he couldn't shake. Three days in Europe: one day in Paris, then two days in Vienna, and he still couldn't shake the jet lag. It probably had something to do with going to bed as soon as they had landed in Paris. This was strictly against Cal's suggestion that they all stay up for the day to allow their bodies to acclimate. But Neil was used to staying up most nights. He had been nocturnal since his college days, so to say that he was surprised at his inability to adapt to the new time zone was an understatement.

Up and down he scrolled again.

"Yeah, I must have just been seeing things." He thought the anomaly was gone. It took another ten minutes to finish his routine, and by then, the smell of fresh-baked bread was wafting in from the main room. Room service had arrived with their food.

Neil clicked his laptop shut and made a mental note to go back later in the day to recheck and thoroughly investigate the anomaly he'd seen. Maybe it was nothing, but with a clearer head, he'd have a chance to analyze it fully. Neil made a mental note to have somebody in Charlottesville take a closer look too.

Then he put the thought aside and went to join his colleagues.

CHAPTER FOUR

Cal and Diane planned to cap off the afternoon with a stop at Notre Dame and took a quick stroll down the Seine; its lazy waters shuttled tour boats along at a leisurely pace. As they wandered, Cal wasn't surprised to see the increased military and police presence. They patrolled in threes and fours, carefully scanning the crowds.

I guess that's just the way it is now, Cal thought. With the ever-present terrorist threat looming, it was impossible for a metropolis like Paris not to be on alert.

The couple walked on, nearing their destination, and merged into the waiting line.

When they entered, Notre Dame impressed them with its high vaulted ceilings, beautiful alcoves for worship, and stained glass windows that had taken years for some poor devil to construct. But what struck Cal most profoundly was that it had taken hundreds of years to reach its current form. That was many times the age of the United States. While America currently stood as a beacon of freedom and democracy to the world, France had been around the game much longer. She and her leaders, dressed in finery and powdered wigs, had once been at the top of the game. And while they were by no means a third world country now, Cal couldn't help but think that all this now stood as remembrance, a reminder of those glory days. Were the golden palaces, the expensive museums, and ancient cathedrals dotting the Paris landscape just a blip on the radar of history? Could they possibly be a lesson to those with the eyes to see and the ears to hear?

Cal agreed with historians that any given country went through fits and starts. Nine times out of ten, a mighty power, like France, Britain, or Spain went through an extended period of nation building and conquering overseas. At least that was how it used to be.

He'd had extensive conversations about world and American history with the president. It was sometimes an uncomfortable thing to think about. America hadn't necessarily planned taking over the Hawaiian Islands, but now they were integral to our nation as a fully integrated state. Today other world powers, like China, were surreptitiously invading places like the African continent. Because of Earth's limited resources, balance was a constant struggle. There were many ways to exert influence. Cal and Brandon had admitted that while a strong America had the ability to be the shining example of righteousness, it didn't always turn out that way. Wrong moves and bad decisions led to very public international declarations that labelled them as "ugly Americans" or the "tyrants that demanded my way or no way."

Brandon equated it to walking a tightrope, where both ends were burning, and in one hand you held the torch of liberty while in the other hand you held a sharp blade. Which way did you walk? Which tool did you use? In government and politics, there were always things you had to do, bills to consider, and someone always had an agenda they wanted to push through Congress. Resting on one's laurels was not an option. It was act or be pushed aside.

Therefore, America's well-earned influence would also ebb and flow, similar to the great nations before it. Its international reputation could be blurred depending on the election cycle, the person sitting in the Oval Office, or the decisions of its Congress.

Cal was thinking about all those things while he visited a country steeped in history. Its people had learned powerful lessons through revolution, under the leadership of possibly one of the world's greatest generals, Napoleon Bonaparte, under the watchful eye of The Church, and more recently, under the evil rule of Nazi Germany.

There was a lesson here, but Cal put it aside. It was a conversation probably best had over a few drinks with Brandon, who more than likely already held the answers. Cal was just coming into his own when it came to considering politics and historical implications. It had taken time and travel to get him philosophizing about such topics. He'd once fancied himself quite one dimensionally as a gun-toting grunt.

But now he had to think about the end game. What would happen if they acted in a certain way? His company, his men, his friends had the power of the President of the United States behind them, but should they disregard the implications, what would the fallout be from their actions? Then they might be the ones flipping the wrong pages of history, the pages that never should have been turned.

"Penny for your thoughts?" Diane said next to him, as they made the turn off the Champs-Elysées. Cal realized he had completely zoned out, and they were nearly back to the hotel.

"I was just thinking about Daniel's friend," Cal lied.

In truth, he had been thinking about that, but not just at that moment.

"Don't tell me you're jealous, Cal."

The Marine laughed. "No, it's nothing like that. I just—you know how Daniel is. This is his world. We are his world, or at least that's what I thought. He's told me some things about his past, but I never wanted to pry. You know what I mean?"

Diane nodded thoughtfully. Daniel had left before the visit to Notre Dame, saying he had to check in with TJG headquarters, but he could have done that anywhere from his phone. They all had secure links back to Charlottesville. Cal suspected there was something deeper going on.

"You don't think it's an old girlfriend, do you?" Diane said.

Cal actually laughed out loud. "Daniel 'Snake Eyes' Briggs, with a girlfriend?" he asked. He was immediately sorry the moment the sarcasm-laced comment left his mouth. In many ways, Daniel had chosen to live an austere life, to be part of The Jefferson Group and nothing else. And yet Cal had never been able to shake the feeling that maybe, just maybe, Daniel might leave them one day, that he had a bigger purpose in this world, and that this was just one more stop in his amazing journey.

He shook his head, "No, I bet it's just an old Marine buddy, er, female buddy."

But as Diane glanced up at him, with a look that conveyed both concern and amusement, Cal couldn't help but think that maybe this new introduction could be a life-altering change for Daniel— a momentous change for all of them.

* * *

LIBERTY, Cal's German Shorthaired Pointer, spun three quick circles next to Cal when they returned to their room. Their hotel didn't usually allow pets, but for a modest fee, almost any request could be accommodated.

"Hello, girl," Cal said bending down to stroke Liberty's chocolate-colored coat, "Have you been a good girl?"

She gazed at him with wide eyes as if she really wanted to speak and tell him: *Yes, I've been a good girl and I haven't gotten into anything, just waited for you.*

"Come on, let me take you outside."

After a quick walk around the block (grass was harder to find in Paris than it was in Charlottesville), they returned to the room. Diane was in the shower, and Cal debated getting in with her. No, there would be time for that later. Besides the tub in the bathroom was elevated and slippery as hell. Who knew what would happen if there were two people in the shower? He'd almost wiped out the first time he'd tried to step out.

While waiting to take his shower, he settled into the armchair in the corner of the room with Liberty at his feet. She always vigilant, like an assassin might slip into the room at any moment. Cal checked his messages, sifted through his emails, and decided that everything at home was safe and secure.

He heard the water turn off in the bathroom, so he rose and shuffled in that direction, stripping down as he went. Liberty knew better than to follow him. She wasn't allowed in the bathroom.

Diane was wrapped in a robe, a towel twisted around her hair, looking in the mirror. Cal snuck in, folded his arms around her, and kissed her on the neck.

"You stink!" she said with mock disgust, while making eye contact in the mirror.

"You smelled the same as me a minute ago," he protested.

Diane shooed him away. "Hurry up and take a shower. I can't wait to meet Daniel's girl."

Cal rolled his eyes, but followed her orders and stepped into the hot shower.

* * *

THEY MET Daniel in the lobby. Cal knew instantly that his friend was off-kilter; Daniel acted like he'd just been put through a tumble dryer. Cal suddenly realized: *He's nervous!*

It was easy to view Daniel Briggs as an immortal man, someone larger than life. Cal had never seen him hurt, or even hesitate in the face of danger. But now, as Diane tried to make small talk with the Marine sniper, Daniel only gave clipped answers and kept glancing toward the hotel door.

The hotel manager, who was doubling as the bartender for the moment, asked if they wanted drinks. Cal ordered a beer while Diane asked for white wine. Daniel mumbled something to the man about wanting a glass of ice water. Diane was trying to pry details from Daniel, and Cal was staring at his discomfited friend. Suddenly, Cal saw Daniel freeze when his eyes roamed to the front door. Cal even thought he detected a slight flush on his friend's features, but then the sniper recovered and took what looked like a steadying breath. Cal turned and saw a striking young woman with straight onyx hair and arctic blue eyes enter the hotel. She was flanked by two men in suits.

She was all high fashion, like she had just stepped off a Paris runway. Her heels click-clacked on the marble floor, and her eyes searched the room. She had brilliant, calculating eyes.

Her eyes finally locked on their little group in the back of the hotel lobby by the bar, and her facial features changed immediately. They were suddenly transformed by a broad smile directed at none other than Daniel Briggs. And then to everyone's surprise, including Daniel's, she actually ran to him and almost leapt into his arms.

Cal's and Daniel's eyes met, and Cal might have read a slight hint of embarrassment in his friend's eyes, but then they closed and Daniel's head eased into the young woman's embrace.

They stood there for a moment. Cal and Diane waited awkwardly for an introduction, but the others were locked together as if they were in their own little world. Cal found himself analyzing the situation. He couldn't remember Daniel ever saying anything about a girlfriend. Maybe a sister, or cousin, but definitely not an old girlfriend. She seemed too young for a girlfriend, and yet there was something about her —a polished, regal bearing.

Finally, the two separated, although the woman maintained a hold on Daniel's arm.

"Hello," the woman said. She must have realized how she appeared, but she didn't seem the least bit embarrassed. She offered a smile that said, *"Oops! Did I just do that in public?"*

"Cal, Diane," Daniel said, "I'd like for you to meet my old friend, Anna Miller."

Anna looked up at Daniel. "It's Varushkin now," she said, "in honor of my grandfather."

Daniel nodded, "Sorry, this is my friend, Anna Varushkin."

Instead of offering a hand, Anna hugged them warmly and greeted them as if she had known them forever. She said, "Daniel has told me so much about you both. It's a pleasure to finally meet you."

She was an American without a hint of an accent. *Well that's a relief*, Cal found himself thinking, *because I haven't heard a thing about you*. But he pushed the negative thoughts away, and tried to focus on the fact that Daniel, for the first time since they had met, seemed truly surprised.

Cal smiled and said, "It's a pleasure to meet you, Anna. I can't wait for you to tell me about my friend Daniel."

CHAPTER FIVE

Gaucho wasn't a museum guy. It probably had something to do with the fact that he'd grown up on the mean streets of Los Angeles and not the posh avenues of New York City. That's why it surprised him how much he was enjoying this trip. Sure, he'd had plenty of chances in the Army to visit new towns, to sample fine foods and to peruse galleries across the globe, but it wasn't until he'd made it through the first floor of the Van Gogh Museum in Amsterdam that he felt something akin to true wonder. It was like a new door had opened in his mind, one that he never knew existed.

It wasn't necessarily the paintings. Gaucho couldn't tell the difference between a Van Gogh and a Picasso. But the fascination was in the way someone had designed the place. It was like reading a story which started following Vincent van Gogh in his late twenties, when he decided to become an artist. Late twenties...not seven or seventeen, but in his late twenties. At that time, being almost thirty and striking out on a new venture was akin to being almost fifty in our times.

From the first floor through the second, Gaucho learned

about Van Gogh's relationship with his brother, that the younger Van Gogh struggled with bouts of depression and uncertainty. Vincent Van Gogh began by copying the masters in an attempt to find his own style.

As they weaved their way through the crowds and up the stairs, Gaucho marveled at the fact that the young Van Gogh had done so much work—hundreds of paintings in a span of ten years. The last year alone, it was said that he painted one painting a day. Even to Gaucho, who had no idea what it took to do such work, he understood that Van Gogh had been something special, if not a bit disturbed.

"Ten years, Top," Gaucho said.

Trent nodded next to him knowingly, like he'd come to the same realization years before and now he was happy that his friend understood the brilliance of it.

"I knew you had to see it," Top said. "Van Gogh might have been a squirrelly bastard, but I believe he was the epitome of putting one's nose to the grindstone."

Gaucho couldn't help but agree. He saw so many correlations with his own work in the military, when he'd run away from home as a teen, shunning the gang lifestyle of his cousins. He'd had no place to go. He'd left home and the Army had embraced him. It had taken his spunk, his pure determination, to turn his life into something else. And he had done it in a dramatic fashion. He'd become a weapon, but a weapon used for good. He'd not only found a vocation, he'd found a new life, something he could be proud of.

Much like Van Gogh and his hundreds of paintings, Gaucho believed that his legacy was something he could leave behind. While Gaucho didn't have a wife and kids to remember him, he had friends like Master Sergeant Willy Trent, Cal Stokes, Daniel Briggs and all the others he'd met and served with through the years. They would remember him no matter what happened.

"Hey, I'm going to go grab a beer from the café, do you want one?" Top asked.

"Give me a few more minutes. I'll meet you there," Gaucho said. He took his time, making his way through that last room, marveling at Van Gogh's use of color, like it wasn't until his final days that the painter had come to use the full spectrum of colors. Gaucho tried to see the inspiration in it, but it was beyond his comprehension. So instead he walked away with the story and the feelings of awe. When he went to the café, Top had yet another meal half devoured in front of him, along with two empty beers. Gaucho knew that he had learned something. He wasn't sure what and he wasn't sure how he would apply it, but he would. He would also pass it along to anyone who would listen.

It was a deeper part of himself that he'd always had, even as a child. He'd never shown it. He never could to those tough street kids. It wasn't that he wanted to be a painter or anything, but for some reason, as he took a seat across from his friend, he felt that his life was irrevocably changed. He couldn't shut that door. And it was all because of a walk-through of a single museum? Gaucho shrugged it off and grabbed the beer that Top had waiting for him.

"So what do you think?" Top asked.

"Pretty cool," Gaucho answered, "Pretty cool."

* * *

TOP WAVED his key ring in front of a sensor at the hotel's glass door. The door opened and the two men stepped inside, waving to the rail thin, model-type desk clerk standing behind the front desk.

"Good afternoon, gentlemen," she said.

There was an older couple making drinks at the honor bar, and they both glanced up at the enormous man passing by. Like he always did, Top grinned at them warmly. His size, and sometimes the color of his skin, had always intimidated people. He found it best to be the first to smile and most times it worked. This time it didn't.

The older woman looked away as if Top had just screamed an obscenity in her face. She grabbed her husband by the crook of the arm and led him away. They had money. Top could see that based on their designer wear and her perfectly coiffed hair.

The men from The Jefferson Group didn't usually stay in places like this, but Cal had told them to spare no expense. He'd put each of them in touch with a travel agent, and she had done the rest. While Top might have preferred to stay somewhere in the middle of the city like he had before, he couldn't deny the simple comforts, like the clean sheets, the big bed, and the hotel's proximity to some of the city's top destinations. He could ignore the snobs along the way.

MSgt. Trent was glad to see that Gaucho had enjoyed the trip so far. His friend was more of the type to have a staycation than go anywhere new. Gaucho was content to crack open a few beers and enjoy a sunset rather than hop a plane to do the tourist thing.

It was something that plagued many former and current operators. They'd seen the world and thought they'd experienced it all. Top's mother had always fostered a sense of curiosity in her son. Although they lived in the worst parts of Atlanta, she still pushed him to learn about the outside world, to appreciate beauty, to think about history, and to understand his place in all of it.

So, it was with genuine happiness that Top understood that he had given his friend Gaucho a gift that day, something his mother had passed along years before, something many men within both his profession and his age group would never see—perspective.

The elevator dinged on the third floor and they tromped down to their room. Both men grew tense as their door came into view. They'd left the Do Not Disturb tag on the handle, but despite that fact, the door was propped open.

No looks were exchanged. They just took up positions on the wall closest to the door and crept their way in, rather than burst in guns blazing. Guns they didn't have. Top knocked on the door. Maybe it was just housekeeping who had ignored the tag.

He thought he'd heard rustling inside; he threw open the door. The place was a mess. Cabinets were thrown open. Sheets and blankets pulled aside. Gaucho rushed in, closing the door behind him.

"They were just here," Gaucho whispered.

Top nodded, pointed to the window and moved that way. When he looked outside, he thought he caught sight of a blur of white in the corner of the courtyard. They were in a residential neighborhood lined by townhouse style homes that sat back-to-back.

Then he saw it again. The blur was now a person. He could tell it was a man by the way the figure moved. *Is he wearing a track suit?*

"He's going that way. White track suit. Dark hair," Top said, thinking he would exit via the window before he realized his frame was too large.

Gaucho must have been thinking the same thing because he said, "You go out the front. I'll go this way," pointing to the window. Without another word, they both bolted for their respective exits. The chase was on.

CHAPTER SIX

The afternoon sessions were going well. This time, it was Jonas's turn to sit in the crowd, and watch as Neil and Dr. Higgins engaged the attendees. "With the advancement of artificial intelligence, the need for human monitoring of computer systems will be minimal," Neil said.

A student in the crowd raised a hand.

"This question is for Dr. Higgins. Dr. Higgins, how do you feel about the migration of human tasks to computers or robotic work systems, as Mr. Patel is saying?"

Dr. Higgins, always thoughtful, gave a slight nod, as if he had just been thinking about that same question. His answer came out slow and measured, the polar opposite of Neil's quick speech.

"I am all for the advancement when it comes to delegating the menial tasks that might take a normal human being tens of hours or even hundreds of hours to do. For example, data mining has grown by leaps and bounds as an industry in the past two decades. By a quick scan around the room, I can see that none of you will remember the days of not having a computer at your fingertips—to not be able to type in a simple query and get any answer that your search engine might provide. If I asked you a question you didn't know the answer to, you'd probably Google it. That type of technology, as long as it remains neutral, can only serve to advance the human race. But I would caution innovators and government leaders alike, not to delegate tasks just for the sake of advancement. I would also postulate that many new industries will be born that necessitate the delicate touch of a living, breathing being. We are humans, after all, and what would this world be without that delicate human touch that we are so used to?"

Jonas had to agree with the doctor. Only a couple years before he might have been on the other side of the argument, he now had come to see the need for a human presence in many areas. For example, in the matter of military direct action, it was easy to say, "Oh, just drop a few bombs on them, and the problem will be fixed," but it was never that easy. Yes, the target might have been obliterated, but what sort of intelligence might have been gleaned if a team of SEALs or even a platoon of Marines had gone in to take down the objective?

Jonas had experienced limited interaction with the military before his time spent with The Jefferson Group and President Zimmer, but now he felt like he had a firm grasp of the concepts creating the new frontier. Drones, while an impressive invention, and undoubtedly convenient, were becoming more of a distraction than the useful tool they were intended as. When an eighteen- or nineteen-year-old kid could sit in Nevada and take out the head of a terrorist organization with his winged weapon, what did that say about humanity? And what did that say about our future?

It had all become so impersonal that soon social networks would be the only way that people would ever interact with one another. No—now Jonas saw it as the stepping-off point.

He had come to believe that younger generations would use it as the first click, and that there would be many revolutions all over the world to essentially de-technologize, returning to day-to-day personal interactions between neighbors and communities sitting face-to-face, rather than using Skype with interactions computer screen to computer screen. That said a lot about Layton's evolvement since he had made his billions in the very world that seemed to be threatening the crux of humanity.

As if reading his mind, Dr. Higgins continued, saying, "Imagine being able to press a button, and all of a sudden, like magic, every single psychological heartache you've ever had was erased, the lessons gone, the feelings disappeared. Now imagine your life after that. Would you be better or worse off? Would it have been better to feel that pain, to learn the lessons, and to come out stronger because of it? The human brain is a magnificent thing. It's been my life's work to study it, to understand it, to learn to harness it fully. Still, I feel as if we don't know much of what we should. Will technology help us get there? Undoubtedly, but I also believe that it will take you and me, looking inside ourselves, to make those discoveries, to share them, to fully experience them. I understand that might not be the in-vogue thing to say, what with all the pills on the market that can make you forget or make you capable of unfeeling." Dr. Higgins exhaled and then smiled. "That's enough preaching from me today. I'm sure you have more questions."

* * *

"I THINK THAT WENT RATHER WELL," Dr. Higgins said, as they walked away from the hotel ballroom that looked like it might have been the center of court for some ancient prince.

"I think you got some people to stop and think, Doc,"

Jonas said. "I know I did, and I love what you said, Neil, about forwarding the cause of technological openness."

Jonas could see that Neil wasn't listening. He was tapping away on his phone. "No, it can't be," he said, almost too quietly for Jonas to hear.

"What is it?" Jonas asked.

"I thought it was a glitch. Why don't you two go ahead? I'll catch up. I need to get back to the room."

"Okay. We'll save you a seat."

Neil nodded, but Jonas could see he wasn't really listening. Neil got that way sometimes, especially when he was working on an important project. When Jonas stopped to think about it, were there really *any* unimportant projects that Neil Patel worked on?

Higgins and Jonas watched him go for a moment, and then Jonas asked, "Hey, Doc, what do you think about mind-reading technology? Is that something we'll see in our lifetime?"

* * *

NEIL RUSHED into the room and grabbed his laptop. Thoughts of cyberattacks—the new incursions of war—flooded his mind. The Russians and the Chinese had become particularly adept at hacking into anything American, but Neil didn't think that those powers were behind this attack.

Attack. The word kept ringing in his head. Neil built the system from the ground up. He knew every aspect of it. He knew every door in, had locked them tight and hidden the keys. But now, instead of using some kind of Trojan Horse, or even a battering ram, something had slipped in through an unseen crack. How was that possible in a closed system?

It might look like nothing had occurred, even to a well-trained eye. But to Neil Patel, the slightest of disturbances screamed incursion. It was like a ghost had stopped by and left the faintest of trails, that only Neil could see.

As he dug deeper into the network, it became crystal clear. Personnel records, surveillance video, and operational flow charts. After his worst fears were confirmed, his stomach felt tied in a knot and his chest tightened. Neil did the only thing he knew possible to stop the data breach utilizing the fail-safe, the ultimate in damage control. He was filled with great reluctance as he typed in the twenty-digit code from memory. Then he watched the entire TJG network go down, and all the memory banks were purged within the blink of an eye.

CHAPTER SEVEN

Cal was no foodie, but he had to admit that he was enjoying the tasting menu. One of the actual owners presented each dish, describing it as lovingly as a parent describes his newborn child. The presentation was beautiful and Cal particularly liked the squid noodles in some broth. He would've asked for more if he'd considered it appropriate. Fortunately, the next course was served before he could ask.

Cal was also enjoying watching the interaction between Anna Varushkin and Daniel. The two bodyguards had left their charge at the hotel. Not a word had been said, but Cal knew that either Anna had prepared them beforehand or, by the looks exchanged, they knew Anna was in good hands with Daniel. Cal wanted answers, not because he didn't trust Daniel's judgment, but because he was genuinely curious about how this girl became involved in his friend's past.

It was the women, Diane and Anna, who commandeered the dinner conversation. They talked of travel and work. Anna was some sort of philanthropist, although she never exactly said what she gave her money to. As the talk flowed, Cal could see that Anna, although young, could probably charm a delegation of granite-faced generals if needed. She had the exuberance of youth and the refinement of royalty. To Cal's amusement, every time she stole a glance at Daniel, the normally stoic sniper flushed just enough for someone who knew him well to recognize.

Oh, how Cal was going to have a field day with Daniel. He felt like he was in sixth grade again, and one of his classmates had been caught holding hands with a girl in the hallway. It wasn't that they had a one-way friendship, but Daniel was always the one with a steady hand on the helm. Now, to see him unsettled—well, it was hard for the Marine in Cal not to want to give Daniel a little bit of barracks grief. It was what friends did, after all.

"You *have* to tell me how you and Daniel met," Diane said, swirling a glass of freshly poured wine much like an expert sommelier.

Anna questioned Daniel with a look; he nodded his response.

"We met in Maine. I was young; Daniel wasn't nearly as well-kempt as he is now." Anna's hand moved to Daniel's collar where she tugged on it playfully. "I was the young, naïve teenager, and he was the protector."

"You never told me you'd been to Maine," Diane said to Daniel. "Was that before or after you got out of the Marine Corps?"

"After," Daniel said. "I was on my ... well, let's just say I was getting myself back together; Anna's family was kind enough to take me in."

Anna laughed but it sounded bitter to Cal's ear.

"My father was a pastor; we lived alone. I thought we had a good life. Like I said, I was naïve. That was my first real lesson in the brutality of life. I guess you could say I walked through fire, but I was lucky enough to have Daniel as my guide. He saved me, and I will be forever grateful."

Anna's and Daniel's eyes were locked now, reliving the memories. For a few beats, the only sound in their quiet corner came from the chatting and clinking of glasses from the rest of the room. Cal almost jumped when Diane jabbed him with her fork under the table.

"Say something," she whispered to him.

Cal searched his mind for the right thing to say but the best thing he could come up with was a blurted, "Daniel never told me he had a girlfriend."

That broke the spell. Both Anna and Daniel looked at him in surprise and then amusement. "Uh, what I meant was ... "

"Is this the part where you give your buddy a hard time because he didn't tell you about some long-lost friend, who just happens to be a girl, sitting next to him at this fine establishment?" Anna asked.

Again, Cal couldn't find the words. She had him. So, it was Diane who answered, "Oh, these boys. They're always doing that. Mention an adult relationship and they run away like little girls with pigtails." Diane tapped on the table, signaling a subject change. "I want to hear more about Russia. Tell me about your family; tell me where they're from."

* * *

THE NIGHT WAS cool but not uncomfortable. The temperature was in the high sixties, possibly the low seventies, but there was a breeze. Both women put their arms around their male companions. Whether it was for the heat or for the comfort, it didn't matter. For those precious moments, they were two contented couples strolling along the Seine in starlit Paris, the Eiffel Tower in the distance.

By the time they got back to the hotel, Cal thought all of

Diane's questions would have been exhausted, yet she kept on, and he could see that she genuinely liked Anna. While she hadn't pressed about her past with Daniel, Cal knew there would be questions later. It was Diane's way. As a naval intelligence officer, she gleaned what she could through passive monitoring and then, like a stealthy ninja, she went in for the attack.

"It was so nice to meet you both," Anna was saying, still holding Daniel's arm in the hotel lobby. This time it was Diane that closed the gap and wrapped her arms around Anna.

"Please come with us tomorrow. I'm taking the boys to the Louvre, and I'm sure you know much more about it than I do."

"Why don't we go instead to the d'Orsay Museum? It's much more manageable. I'm afraid the boys might get lost if we go through the Louvre. Maybe save it for another day," Anna suggested.

"Sold," Diane said, letting go of her new friend. "And now, if you'll excuse me, I think I'll take my man upstairs. He owes me a foot massage for wearing these painful high heels." Diane was already barefoot, the black torture devices hanging from her index finger. "Goodnight, Anna. Goodnight, Daniel," she said as she headed for the elevator.

"It was a pleasure meeting you, Anna," Cal said, hugging her goodbye. "Don't keep Daniel out too late, okay? He promised to go on a run with me in the morning."

Anna made an X over her heart and held up two fingers. "On my honor, Mr. Stokes."

* * *

THEY DECIDED to go for a walk. Daniel wasn't tired, and it didn't feel like Anna was leaving any time soon. The tidal wave of emotions washing through him was something that he hadn't felt in years.

He'd kept in touch with Anna and her family. Years before he had attended the funeral for her grandfather—the great Georgy Varushkin. He'd been shocked to see the woman Anna had become. Halfway through dinner Daniel was forced to admit that Anna was the most beautiful woman he'd ever seen. Every little thing that had been intriguing about her as a child was only enhanced now, made better, like a fine wine aged perfectly. Anna had come into her own.

Her precocious inquisitiveness as a teen had blossomed into a refined curiosity about the world. For a while they walked arm in arm without talking, and for Daniel it was better that way. The man who was afraid of nothing was suddenly afraid he'd say the wrong thing. Part of him still saw her as a child. Strong, no doubt, but still a child. Then, when he glanced at her, he saw the woman she'd become, and it filled him with the nervousness of a high school teen, or a Marine on leave who'd seen his first pretty girl in a foreign land.

"I really like your friends," Anna said. "When do you think they'll get married?"

Daniel was happy for the question especially because it wasn't about him. "Sometime soon, I hope. They're good together. I've never seen Cal so happy."

"You told me he was engaged before and that he lost his fiancée."

Daniel nodded. "That was before I met him. It hung over him for a long time, but Diane surprised him. She stood up to him in a way no woman had done before. For Cal that was a big deal. He respects her strength. They're good for each other."

"And you?" Anna asked. "What are you looking for in Mrs. Right?"

Daniel was amazed to find that the words couldn't find their way past his dry throat.

"You don't have to answer," Anna said, much to Daniel's relief. She hugged him tighter and Daniel didn't know if it was because of the wind that had just kicked up along the Champs-Elysées or if it was something else. He was almost afraid to hope for that something else.

They walked along in silence again, Daniel thinking about the path his life had taken. He was in a good place. He felt that he was the best he'd ever been, and then Anna had walked in to that hotel lobby and taken his perfect snow globe life and shaken it with the power of the universe.

Get yourself together; she's just a kid, Daniel thought to himself.

A few seconds later he was about to apologize for the awkwardness when the phone in his pocket buzzed. He thought that maybe it was Cal calling to confirm their morning run, but it was Neil.

"Hey, I couldn't get Cal," Neil's voice was panicky.

"What is it?" Daniel asked, drawing a curious gaze from Anna.

"It's gone. It's all gone," Neil said, the anxiety rising in his voice.

"Slow down," Daniel said. "What's gone?"

Neil was babbling something, but Daniel didn't understand the techno jargon of Neil thinking out loud.

"Neil, take a breath. Tell me what happened."

He heard Neil take a ragged breath, slow and unsteady. Then he told Daniel what had happened.

"Are you sure?" Daniel asked.

"I'm sure."

"Okay, I'll let Cal know," Daniel said as he ended the call.

"Is everything all right?" Anna asked.

"We need to get back to the hotel," Daniel said. "I'm sorry to cut our night short but .... "

Anna shook her head, "It's okay. You should go."

"Will you be all right?"

Anna pointed to a row of cabs along the road. "I'll be fine." Then she stood up on her toes and kissed him on the cheek. "Call me when you can."

Daniel nodded and without another word turned on his heel and sprinted to the hotel.

CHAPTER EIGHT

It was as if the dog could sense that something was wrong, very wrong. As Diane busied herself packing their belongings, Cal sat on the bed digesting the information that Daniel had just brought. The first knock had been soft, but the second knock held more urgency. At first Cal hadn't answered because, well, what else was there to do after a romantic evening in Paris? He slipped out of bed, somehow found his pants before answering the door, and there was Daniel, back to his calm, assured normal again, despite the news he delivered.

Immediately, they agreed they would not use any electronics unless absolutely necessary. If someone had hacked into Neil's system, they were good—very good—and there was no need to tempt that fate by using seemingly secure lines that could be tapped as well. As Cal sat there absently stroking Liberty's head to calm her, his mind flipped between options about where they'd erred. Nobody had ever gotten into Neil's systems before. Well, except for that nasty little business in Jackson Hole, Wyoming. It wasn't just the systems they'd gotten into; they'd gotten into Neil.

"Nick Ponder," Cal murmured.

"What was that?" Diane asked.

"Huh? Oh, nothing. I was just thinking out loud."

But Ponder was dead. Long gone, buried in a nondescript grave on some mountain in Wyoming; no, not Wyoming. He'd been killed overseas. Cal had forgotten that detail. There had been so many deaths since then, including the death of his own cousin, Travis Hayden. Travis had been the president's chief of staff at the time. Cal's mind was wandering now. It snapped back into place at the realization that their reliance on technology had taken them down. It was easy to say that Neil, being the techie genius that he was, could never be hacked, but the seemingly impossible had happened. Now the entire team was scrambling to figure out what they should do. Everyone knew the dire circumstances TJG was in - all except Top and Gaucho.

Daniel ran down to a local store and purchased a burner phone, then tried to contact their friends in Amsterdam, but received no answer. They could take care of themselves, but it still worried Cal and Daniel. This had been a deliberate attack and it was only through Neil's quick actions that The Jefferson Group's most vital information hadn't been leaked. At least that's what Neil said, but at the moment Cal didn't believe it. He had to plan for the worst so, much to his dismay, he realized who he would have to call now.

* * *

"So what's next on the agenda?" the president asked.

Marge "The Hammer" Haines, the president's new chief of staff looked down at the daily itinerary. "We have about ten minutes of down time and then it's over to the Department of Justice to talk to the attorney general."

"Again, why couldn't he come here?" the president asked.

"You offered to go there," Haines said, wryly.

"Right, and you told me that I shouldn't." The attorney general was one of the last hangers-on from the old administration. In truth, President Zimmer wanted to make the trip as a way of extending an olive branch. It would also give him a firmer sense of the current attorney general's focus and goals, hopefully helping the president decide whether to keep the AG on for another term.

"Right, I forgot."

"Do you ever miss it?" Zimmer asked.

"Miss what?" Haines said, not looking up from her phone to which she was permanently glued.

"Running SSI." SSI stood for Stokes Security International, a company formed by Cal's own father, Earl Calvin Stokes, Sr., while the younger Cal was still in high school. Marge had been the company's first female CEO before coming to Washington to work with the president.

"I miss being in better shape," Marge said, looking up at the president.

Not for the first time, Zimmer realized how strikingly beautiful the attorney was. Add to that her quick wit, sharp mind, and ruthless common sense, and Marge Haines was a force to be reckoned with. Haines looked back to her phone first, and the president wondered if she thought he was staring at her. He had to remember not to do that. She worked for him now, and although she'd become a very good friend, much like her predecessor, Travis Hayden, there still had to be a clear line between them. They worked closely together, day in and day out, and the last thing the president wanted was to complicate things.

"Right. Travis used to tell me stories about you, how you'd go down to the gym and take out a squad of SSI guys."

Haines laughed. "Did he really tell you that?"

They could talk about Travis now. The throbbing pain was

still there, sometimes acute, but they'd learned to live with it. Some days they felt Travis's very real presence within the Oval Office, still watching over things the way the former SEAL had done in life.

"Maybe it wasn't a squad. Fire team?" the president said with a grin.

Haines shrugged. "I don't think I could do that now. I feel like all my sharp edges are getting chewed away by this place."

It struck the president that Haines hadn't denied taking down four men in hand-to-hand combat. He'd heard the rumors. Travis and even Cal said that "The Hammer," as Haines was called behind her back, was deadly in the court-room, but she could also absolutely hold her own against a man twice her size and trained for war. He chalked that up as one more thing to admire about the woman.

A buzzing from inside the Resolute Desk shook the president from his thoughts, thankfully. He reached inside the middle drawer and pulled out the phone Cal had given him. One would think that the communications of the President of the United States would be secure, that the White House had a shell impenetrable to foreign powers, but precautions still had to be taken. Technically, the relationship between the president and The Jefferson Group was beyond the scope of what the leader of the free world and a private company should be. If word of it leaked out ... well, that couldn't happen.

That had necessitated linking through another means, more specifically one of Neil Patel's specially-made phones. Zimmer didn't understand the technology, at least not completely, but he trusted Neil. He'd never failed, and neither had his technology. So, when he answered the call, the president fully expected a routine conversation. Everyone from The Jefferson Group was on vacation, after all. It had been the president's suggestion. More than a suggestion. It was an order from a commander taking care of his troops. Cal and the team deserved the time off. The president had to admit, with some satisfaction, that he'd gotten a kick out of Diane making Cal choose where they went on their trip.

"Hey, Cal. I'm here with Marge," the president said, tilting back in his chair. The president had to strain to hear Cal's reply. Even then, he still couldn't make it out completely.

"Say that again?" Zimmer asked, putting the phone back in handset mode so he could hear. Cal repeated his report and the president felt his body freeze involuntarily. He looked up at Haines, who was still fixated on her phone. "I understand," Zimmer said, and he ended the call.

"Well, that was quick," Haines said. "Let me guess, Cal wanted to call and rub it in our face that he got time off and we were stuck here in the Oval Office, kissing politician's asses while the rest of them eat baguettes and French cheese?"

The president didn't even hear her. *It can't be,* he thought. Things had been progressing in exactly the direction he and Cal had planned. The Jefferson Group was quite possibly the president's most treasured tool. That could be because he knew the men—really knew the men. They were his friends, he spent time with them, bled with some of them. It felt like he was one of them, something akin to a military unit that had spent years fighting the enemy together. Cal's words had caught him off guard.

Zimmer hadn't thought it was possible. Anything was possible of course, but this?

"Mr. President?" Haines was asking. From the look on her face it wasn't the first time she'd tried to get his attention, and the fact that she was calling him Mr. President while they were alone said it all.

His brain bounced with the first signs of his body going

into damage control. He fixated on two words Cal had said. Two words. *How could two words pack so much punch?* He broke them down one by one. The first word was an homage to Travis Hayden's gift to his cousin. He'd bought the puppy, a German Shorthaired Pointer, from a breeder in the Midwest. Months after Travis's death, the dog had been given to Cal, and she'd become the official mascot of The Jefferson Group. Not long after, the dog's name, Liberty, had become their call sign.

Liberty. The word echoed in his mind. It was supposed to be a positive word. Something so American, so apple pie, that none could mistake it. *Liberty*, his mind repeated again. And then the next word shot out like a dagger, killing the first with savage glee.

"Liberty Down," Zimmer finally said.

"What did you say?" Haines asked.

Zimmer looked up from his desk where he realized his hands lay, shaking.

"Liberty Down. Someone's taken down The Jefferson Group."

CHAPTER NINE

Ian Rourke was pleased. His operation had been months in the making, and while a normal man might have chafed at the long hours of surveillance, many of which he took himself, despite being president of the company, Rourke enjoyed the process. It was long and tedious to be sure, but always fruitful in the end.

Everyone had secrets. That was one thing he'd learned, first as a cop and then as a special agent with the Bureau. His company specialized in digging out those secrets. Like veins in a gold mine, they always led to more gold.

Rourke was still amazed that even when confronted with the truth, so many outed targets were shocked to see that they posted their own ending on social media, or in an email that had found its way into the wrong hands. There were certain precautions that could be taken, but Rourke had learned to avoid the pitfalls completely. Face-to-face was always the best way. Of course, there were surveillance companies like his roaming the world, working for bidders high and low. He'd seen traces of his competition over the years: a smashed piece of chalk on a busy city street, or a magnetic key box still stuck to the bottom of a phone booth. Those were two tried and true techniques for spies brought up in the Cold War Era. They, in turn, passed them on to later generations. The old stuff still worked; it was tried and true for a reason.

Yes, technology had its place, and Rourke's company augmented its rough street style with the newer instruments of his profession: incursion software, long range mics and the best optics money could buy. But the most significant way Rourke and his company separated themselves from the others was their patience.

Investigations could take months, and this one had been no exception. His target, a seemingly innocuous company based in Charlottesville, Virginia, The Jefferson Group, had been an interesting challenge. He'd never heard of it until Congressman McKnight had mentioned it to him in that hotel room, but now he knew so much. With facial recognition software readily available on the open market, it had been easy to figure out the main players.

There was Dr. Alvin Higgins, a former employee of the Central Intelligence Agency, and, according to Rourke's contacts, possibly the best interrogator in the world. There had been awe, maybe a little bit of jealousy in his contact's voice as he told Rourke of Higgins' past exploits. If even half of them were true, Higgins was indeed the best.

And then there was Neil Patel, a graduate of the University of Virginia. He'd spent a decade or so after graduation with SSI, Stokes Security International, mostly in their Nashville, Tennessee headquarters. But he'd also spent time at their dual headquarters just outside of Charlottesville. He was a public figure to a certain degree, well known for his innovations. He had licenses with high-tech industries and with the military. Rourke estimated his net worth in the hundreds of millions of dollars. There was no way to be sure of course, but an estimate would suffice. Rourke's estimates were almost always spot on.

An interesting inclusion in the small group was Jonas Layton, aka, The Fortune Teller. He'd made his billions concocting predictions that others found ridiculous and maybe even self-aggrandizing at the time, but the world had come to see that Layton was a true forward thinker. He was a man who could see into the future with the clarity of a bright summer day. His services were sought out by startups, venture capital funds, and government agencies. Who wouldn't want a whiz kid like Layton on their side?

The former Marine, gigantic though gregarious Willy Trent stood out the most, at least physically. A simple internet search had dug up the fact that he was once a highly touted NFL prospect, but instead of entering college and moving on to the draft, he'd enlisted in the Marine Corps and eventually made his way to TJG.

The short Hispanic, the one with the funny braided beard and Trent's constant companion, was the one they called "Gaucho." He'd been one of the hardest to crack. Rourke's people tracked his family back to Los Angeles and even found a GED from the man's high school years, but then the trail had gone cold. At first, Rourke had thought that maybe the burly Mexican was some sort of criminal, but then an enlistment certificate was produced in St. Louis. Unearthed next were the discharge papers after fifteen years of service but there was not a single entry during that time. That told Rourke that this Gaucho was the elite of the elite, possibly even Delta Force. He had to respect that.

The two men who intrigued Rourke the most, might not have seemed like the leaders of the company; after all, Layton was TJG's public face. First there was Daniel Briggs, a quiet figure, always in the background, but Rourke had seen from the pictures and the video, combined with his own personal surveillance, that Briggs was something else. His records indicated that Briggs was a Marine sniper. He had never been wounded in combat, and it had taken a call to the head of the RNC to dig up the fact that Briggs had been up for the Medal of Honor. The award had simply disappeared. It had not been downgraded to a Navy Cross or even a silver star, it had just been pulled. Poof, it was gone. But Rourke had read what Briggs had done, how many men he'd killed. The man was a hero, no doubt, but heroes didn't sway Rourke one way or the other.

He had a job to do and the way he saw it, the last man, Cal Stokes, was the key. Cal was the son of Colonel Calvin Stokes, Sr., United States Marine Corps, retired, and founder of SSI. Stokes was a one-time student at the University of Virginia who enlisted shortly after 9/11. Stokes had made his bones on the battlefields of Afghanistan and Iraq. He'd walked away with a Navy Cross, one step below the vaunted Medal of Honor. That, while special, wasn't completely rare, and just a footnote for Rourke. What most intrigued him was a series of articles published a few years before in Nashville. One had even made national news due to Stokes's history with the Marines. The articles detailed a brutal attack in Nashville. Stokes's fiancé had been killed, but in the process, Stokes had killed four men and maimed another. There were no interviews, but there had been witnesses.

Even that story wasn't what most impressed Rourke. It was the fact that after the attack, not only had the culprit of the attack, Dante West, disappeared, but so had Stokes. There was the usual trail of personal data, bank accounts, mortgages, all normal activity, but professionally, Stokes had disappeared. No trace in the government records he accessed or any public database. Then, out of the blue, The Jefferson Group had been formed by Jonas Layton and *voilà*, just like that, Cal Stokes reappeared.

Rourke didn't believe in coincidences, and he now knew after much examination, that the collection of so many elite personalities, was not by chance. But even as he watched them, he'd known it would be close to impossible to break into their inner circle. The men of The Jefferson Group were careful. They watched their moves like well-trained Dobermans. That had necessitated a higher level of vigilance on Rourke's part, but it was not unexpected.

What had come as fully unexpected, was the fact that Rourke respected these men, not for what they'd done or who'd they'd become. There were any number of men and women around the world with more impressive resumes. It was the fact that they were now hiding in plain sight, using their position with complete anonymity instead of concealing themselves, much like Rourke's company. They almost flaunted who they were, but they were still in business, meaning they were very good at what they did. They were experts in their fields, some of the best, and that intrigued Rourke.

It wasn't until by some stroke of luck the entire headquarters element of The Jefferson Group left to go on vacation, giving Rourke's people their shot. They'd gotten in. It wasn't easy, but they'd done it. Because of the sensitive nature of the operation and his connection to McKnight, Rourke was the only one who had seen it all. He was impressed.

This Neil Patel had been careful and had covered their tracks well, but Rourke put the pieces together. The cog, the shining jewel of this treasure, was the fact that he'd made the connection, the one that McKnight had asked for. These warriors, these men of The Jefferson Group weren't just friends of the president—they were working for him. If America and the world could see what the president's friends had been up to—well, that wasn't Rourke's job.

As he sat in a Paris apartment, overlooking the hotel in

which Cal Stokes and his girlfriend Diane were staying, Rourke wondered where this investigation would lead. He knew that his sabotage of the small company had only been a slap in the face and they'd already compartmentalized the problem.

It was the politicians who would do the real damage, and if he knew anything about McKnight, Rourke had no doubt that despite his congenial relationship with the president, he would take the information Rourke provided and use it to secure the ultimate prize, the best seat in the house, the mansion on Pennsylvania Avenue.

CHAPTER TEN

"How could this happen?" Neil wondered, his fingers flying back and forth between two laptops.

"You shouldn't blame yourself," Dr. Higgins said, but even he couldn't hide the concern in his voice.

"Whoever did this is *good*," Neil said, "I can't find a trace of where they came from."

The whole system had already been shut down. It was the worst-case scenario in Neil's mind. Not only had it been shut down, it had also been scrubbed. Now, it would be difficult to prove The Jefferson Group had ever existed, except someone had hacked in and would have that evidence.

"We should have stayed in Paris. Cal would know what to do."

"We have to take care of ourselves, Neil. We should leave, NOW."

Higgins had explained his larger concerns. If the hackers had gained entry into Neil's system, they had probably been followed. The locations of the members of The Jefferson Group were most likely known. That meant all members were in real physical danger.

Jonas burst into the room. "I got us a flight, but we need to go *now*!"

"Wait, I'm not done here—Where are we going?" Neil asked.

"Zurich first and then to Morocco," Jonas said, snatching his overnight bag from the bed.

"Morocco? Why Morocco?"

"I've got some friends there that won't ask questions," Jonas explained.

Neil reluctantly stowed his computers and gathered his things. He felt like the third wheel now; he felt worthless without his robust computer arsenal in his hands. No, not worthless, but he felt he imposed a burden on the team. He'd gotten cocky. They'd been lucky over the years. At that moment, he promised himself if they got through this, he would be more careful—infinitely more careful. He would be like Daniel - always vigilant.

At first he really had thought that maybe it was a blind incursion, that TJG's network had been swept up in some random search. But as he dug, he found that it was much more insidious. It had been pinpoint targeted. He was left with only one choice. Although of devastating consequence, he had to shut it all down.

"Okay, I'm ready to go," Neil said, bags over each shoulder. He'd never been a light packer.

"Leave your clothes," Dr. Higgins instructed, "We can always get replacements later."

Neil looked at him incredulously.

"But that's all my stuff."

That was when Neil noticed that the only thing the other two men carried were simple satchels. Oh, he'd missed that. Where were their bags?

"We can buy things when we get there," Higgins urged, making his way to the door. Neil went to the closet and deposited his bag on the suitcase stand. As the seconds ticked by, the danger began to feel more imminent and more real.

Dr. Higgins had been the one to take the lead in their small group. Of the three men, Higgins was the one with the most operational experience. It was sometimes easy to forget that fact. Higgins looked like a tenured professor, more accustomed to the college faculty cocktail hour and hours-long discussions with his students. Whatever trepidation Neil felt, he tried to tamp it down with the thought that Higgins was used to this. As if to put an exclamation point on that fact, Neil remembered that Higgins was the only one armed.

"Neil, it's time," Higgins said. Neil hadn't realized that he'd been daydreaming, imagining Higgins in some faraway land, getting the scum of the earth to spill their guts.

"I'm coming," Neil said, his spirits once again uplifted.

Higgins opened the door slowly and peeked out into the hallway. It must have been clear, because he opened it wide and ushered the other two out of the room. After slipping the *Do Not Disturb* tag onto the doorknob, Higgins followed them to the elevator.

"We should take the stairs," he said.

It was another fact that Neil failed to consider, although he remembered Cal once saying that elevators were death traps. You never wanted to get caught in one, because there really was no way out, despite what you saw in the movies.

His apprehension spiked again, and he had to grab the strap of his bag tight to prevent his hands from shaking. Neil had had his own close call before. He'd been kidnapped and tortured, and to this day, he still had night-mares about his capture. He would never admit it, but it haunted him; it would always hang over him. And now that there was a chance that men with guns were coming to get him, he felt that familiar dread creep into his body, like a snake wrapping its way slowly around, slithering for Neil's neck.

They rushed down the stairs. Neil was careful to hold the handrail. He felt so unsteady. When they got to the lobby, no one was there except a maid vacuuming the carpet by the bar. She didn't even look up as they hurried past. As the delicious cool night air hit Neil's face, he closed his eyes and inhaled. They were going to make it. He was beginning to believe that.

A black Mercedes pulled up curbside, and Jonas was about to slip in when a wail of sirens nearby made them all look up. Suddenly they were surrounded by police cars. There were lights flashing and more sirens blaring.

Without even realizing it, Neil put his hands in the air. His mind went to the worst. Somebody had gotten to the Vienna police. In Neil's mind, that made it worse. If they'd gotten to the authorities, who knew how far up the opposition was? At least he'd had the foresight to wipe his laptops clean.

Strong hands grabbed him by the arms, shoving him into the back of a waiting cruiser. Neil strained and saw Jonas getting the same treatment. But Dr. Higgins got the worst of it, because they had found his gun. No less than three policemen had the doctor pinned to the ground like he was some sort of terrorist. Neil wanted to scream at them, to tell them they were wrong, that they had made a mistake. But he couldn't get the words past his lips. He was caged, and the dread that had been creeping upon him minutes before now seized him as the anaconda tightened its stranglehold.

"Where are you taking us?" he managed to ask the officer sitting in the front. The man ignored him, so Neil asked again, "Please? Tell me what we've done wrong? Where are you taking us?"

The police officer didn't even turn around to acknowledge

Neil. He shifted the car from park into drive. Neil wanted to yell at the man to get an answer, any answer. He wanted to bang on the partition, but his hands felt small and ineffectual. He wasn't cuffed, but he felt tied down, rooted to the spot. It wasn't until the police car fell in line with the rest of the convoy that the officer spoke.

"Relax, Mr. Patel," he said, "As long as you cooperate, you will come out of this just fine."

It wasn't the words that frightened Neil. It was the fact that the words had come out easily, and not in accented English of a Viennese native. The words were spoken by an American ... an American dressed in an Austrian police officer's uniform.

CHAPTER ELEVEN

"There could be six of them watching the building," Daniel said, "Maybe more."

Daniel had returned with a bag of groceries that he put on the side table when he entered the hotel room.

"We should wait until after midnight," Daniel said, "It will give us the best chance of getting out undetected."

Even as he said it Daniel didn't quite believe it. He'd been negligent but rather than chastise himself like Cal was doing, Daniel would analyze the situation and try to find a way out of the puzzle box. Whoever had done this was very good. Daniel suspected they'd kept their distance, which was smart if they knew which hotel they were staying in. It was easy to monitor from afar. It was like posting Marine snipers kilometers from an objective, impossible to detect but deadly accurate in their vision of the battlefield.

That's how Daniel would have done it. Stake out a few positions in and around buildings in the area: whatever would give clear views of every way in and out. No roving patrols unless absolutely necessary. The surveillance teams didn't have to get close, not with the wide boulevards in

Paris and the predictable routes of three vacationing tourists.

How many cars were parked on each side of the local streets, owners chatting away on their phones? Any one of a thousand of them could have been watching, and Daniel and Cal never would have known.

"Then we wait," Cal said, putting his hand over Diane's.

If she was worried, she didn't show it. For a fleeting moment, it made Daniel think that he wanted Anna there too. He recoiled from a pang of longing that was so unfamiliar he wondered how it had gotten there. In truth, he didn't want her to get mixed up in this.

He'd been able to get word to her by borrowing an old man's phone on the street. Anna insisted that she could help, but Daniel had said no. He told her it was too dangerous for her, she should leave and he would contact her later.

Their goodbye had been short and it left a bitter taste in Daniel's mouth, but he thought it was totally necessary. The more he'd had time to think about it, the more Daniel realized that Anna now held some special place in his heart. While that might have been perfect on a sunny day strolling through Paris, it could impact operational decisions in a way that could get them all killed. Daniel wouldn't let that happen. Indeed, he *couldn't* let that happen. He only hoped that Anna had listened to him and that her security had already whisked her far from Paris.

"So you think we should take the train?" Cal asked.

Daniel nodded. "The airport's too risky and there's no chance of renting a car at this time of night. At least at the station, we can see them coming."

Liberty stood up from where she was sitting at Cal's feet and walked over to Daniel. She licked his hand as if to ask, "What's my part in all this?"

Daniel bent down and stroked her back.

"Will Anna be okay?" Diane asked.

"She'll be fine," Daniel said, "she's probably half way to London by now. She's a smart girl, and she's not without her own resources. Besides, she's been through worse."

"I really liked her, Daniel," Diane said. "I'm sorry this happened. Maybe we can get together again after we figure out what's going on."

Daniel found it odd that Diane was worried about match-making at a time like this. He thought that maybe she should be worried about something else - like their safety.

Then he realized that he'd been worrying about the same thing so he said, "I'm sure we'll see her soon."

* * *

JUST ACROSS THE STREET, Ian Rourke was reading his scattered teams' most recent reports. One confirmed the apprehension of the three subjects in Vienna. Rourke wasn't sure what he was going to do with the men in custody, but that decision would be up to McKnight. Rourke was still personally monitoring the trio with the dog across the way.

The two in Amsterdam had disappeared. His team leader reported to Rourke that there had been a chase after their contractor had been spotted. The local contact had slipped away, but the pursuing team had missed the opportunity.

Rourke wasn't worried. Amsterdam was a small city and there were only so many ways in and out. Even if Trent and Gaucho slipped through his net, it wasn't the end of the world. He had all he really needed. The initial pull from TJG's network was the prize. Gathering the guilty parties was just icing on the cake.

Rourke perused the pictures on his tablet, including the latest batch of surveillance footage from Paris. He hadn't had time to go over it earlier and was just getting caught up on the day's activity when he froze. He zoomed in on the picture. He looked again. Then he shook his head.

Rourke flipped to the next shot. This one was clearer. It was an image of a young woman with straight black hair. She looked so familiar. Rourke hadn't been on scene when it was taken, and he'd initially only read the report that Stokes, Briggs and the Mayer girl had been joined by another woman. At the time, he'd brushed it off as a friend of the companions, but now as he examined the picture of a familiar face, something twisted in Rourke. He swore he recognized her.

He flipped to the next picture, the clearest so far. Then there was no doubt. It was who he thought it was. *"Anna Varushkin,"* he muttered to himself in shock.

The memories flooded back. At the end of his time with the FBI, Rourke had been part of the top-secret team tasked with working with Anna's grandfather, Georgy, founder and head of an organization called The Pension. The Pension had been responsible for filtering billions of dollars out of Russia and smuggling hundreds of Russian dissidents to the U.S. Many of the refugees were former Russian government officials, military leaders and their families who'd been on the receiving end of Russia's new regime. Georgy himself had spent years in a Russian gulag.

In the eyes of the American government, there was nothing wrong with what Georgy Varushkin and his countrymen had done. It was the United States of America, after all, and the powers that be recognized the advantage of having the well-connected refugees on their side. Thus, a bargain was struck, and the Russian-turned Americans were allowed to keep their money and given assistance in establishing their own communities.

That did not mean that someone wouldn't keep an eye on the Varushkin clan. The FBI had been tasked with maintaining the relationship and handling surveillance. As a seasoned veteran, Rourke had been one of the FBI's liaisons.

In exchange for added protection from the FBI and a select group of government agencies, Georgy and his people provided intelligence, and kept tabs on the inner workings of the Russian government and the Russian economy. It was a valuable relationship, and Rourke, who'd at first been put off by the assignment, had grown to admire the elder Varushkin. By that time, the Varushkin patriarch was bound to a wheelchair, courtesy of his years spent in a Russian prison.

Rourke now remembered the first time he'd seen Anna. She was so full of life and every bit Georgy's granddaughter. They were inseparable, and when she'd bounded into the room that day, barely twenty at the time, Rourke had felt a flutter in his chest.

It wasn't just the fact that she was beautiful and intelligent. She had a way of brightening the darkest room, and as his assignment with The Pension progressed, Rourke found himself scheduling his own time with the family so he might see Anna. He was too professional to make advances, but he'd been drawn to her, like a lonely sailor to a distant lighthouse, its presence both irresistible and lifesaving.

She was innocent and kind, something Rourke, who came from a broken home, had never experienced. It not only surprised him, but also it gave him hope. So, he'd done everything in his power to make sure the Varushkins were protected, ensuring members of the Russian mob and the Russian government never got close enough to touch either Anna or her grandfather. They had tried, but Rourke and his compatriots thwarted every attempt.

That had been years ago, and yet, as he stared at the picture, Rourke felt those familiar feelings flood back like stepping into a rainbow and having the rest of the world wash away.

Rourke's mind snapped back to the present. What was Anna doing here? Why was she with Stokes and Briggs?

It didn't make sense. Nothing in their files connected them to the Varushkin family. As he flicked through more pictures, Rourke realized it was more than just coincidence. Anna knew them, or at least knew the Briggs character. He could see it in her body language. She cared for him.

Rourke was too old to be jealous, but he was concerned. He was too far down the rabbit hole to stop now. McKnight's orders had been clear, and Rourke had never before failed on a mission. He'd never failed to deliver.

When Rourke saw the lights of the car out of the corner of his eye, he looked out the window to see a black SUV pull to the curb in front of the hotel. A moment later, Anna stepped out. Rourke had a decision to make, but his memories of the past assaulted him as Anna hurried into the hotel. He wondered how he was going to protect her from the upcoming mayhem.

CHAPTER TWELVE

Anna said a silent prayer as she rushed into the lobby, nodding to the man at the front desk as she flew by. Daniel had told her to leave, and she almost had. There was even a helicopter waiting for her at the airport, but she'd ordered her driver to turn back. She couldn't leave now.

She lived a fulfilling life. She traveled as often as she liked. She was able to help people stranded far from their homeland, forced to leave because of the tyrannical rule of the Russian government. They looked to her as their leader, despite her youth. They'd respected her grandfather, and now they respected her. They were a family and she took that responsibility seriously. But while the role of keeper of The Pension kept her busy in day-to-day management, there'd always been something missing.

Anna always knew that she'd be married at some point. None of the young men who came calling ever fit what she considered to be the perfect man. Not that perfection was what she expected, but Anna always had that vision, that image of the person who would complete her, who could be her other half, who could challenge her but be there for her.

He would understand who she was and from where she'd come.

She'd lived for years with the blissful belief that her father was a perfect man. She'd put him on a pedestal and then she'd found out the truth. It'd been built on a foundation of lies. Anna hadn't known it at the time, and in fact it had been long after Daniel's departure from Boston all those years ago that her grandfather had finally told her the truth. Her father was no hero. He'd been the worst of all people. He'd betrayed her, and he'd betrayed the family. And what had he done it for? Money and power: two things he railed against in his weekly sermons.

Anna hadn't left her room for three days after finding out, but when she finally emerged, she had become a woman.

And yet now, as she opened the hidden door that looked like a bookcase and took the steps three at a time, Anna felt like an awkward teenager again, making a rash decision without fully thinking. But she *had* thought about it and she couldn't let that thought go.

When Daniel opened the door, his face was tight. It wasn't what she'd expected.

"You shouldn't be here Anna. I told you it wasn't safe," he'd said.

"I don't care. I want to be here with you, and if I can help, well, I'm here to help."

Daniel stared at her for a long moment and then his face relaxed, flashing her an understanding smile, allowing her to breathe once again. Instead of saying anything, he wrapped her in his arms, and she thought she might cry. She held it all in, hugging him in return, thinking that she'd been foolish to put him in an awkward position. Again, the thought came that they might be in danger, but she didn't care. She'd been in danger before. She'd been kidnapped by her own mother.

As long as she was with Daniel, she would be safe. She knew that.

A moment later the door opened and something brushed past her leg. It was Liberty, Cal and Diane's dog. She was running circles around Anna and Daniel, her tail straight as an arrow.

"Oh, I'm sorry. I didn't know," Cal stuttered as he came to the doorway, Diane right behind him.

Anna let Daniel go and composed herself.

"It's okay. It's my fault," she said.

"You really shouldn't be here Anna," Cal said seriously, scanning the room as if someone were about to jump out of the shadows. Anna processed the thoughts in her head, struggling to find the syllables so she could explain to them.

But it was Diane who answered first.

"She's not leaving," Diane said. That wonderful woman walked up to Anna and wrapped a protective arm around her. "We've just gotten to be good friends. We can't ask her to leave now."

"This is ridiculous," Cal said through gritted teeth. "I should send you both back to the States right now."

"But you can't," Diane snapped, "and that's that. So instead of complaining about it, why don't you tell us what you have in mind to save the day."

Cal glared at her for a long moment and Anna really thought that there was anger there. Then Cal's face mellowed. "Suit yourselves, but she needs to know what she's getting into. Daniel, you tell her."

Daniel told Anna about the surveillance teams, about the company network that had been infiltrated and then taken down. A strange calm came over Anna as she listened. It was the same feeling she got whenever there was a crisis on hand. Her mind cleared as the picture solidified like a movie screen fading in after the opening credits.

When Daniel had finished the story, Anna asked, "How long do you think they've been watching you?"

Cal's head snapped back to the conversation, "What does that matter?"

Anna shrugged, "It could give us some indication of who might be doing it. I'm sure from what Daniel's told me that there are any number of organizations who would like to see your organization dismantled." She felt Diane squeeze her hand in reassurance. It pushed her on even through Cal's and Daniel's stares. "Let me help, please. I promise I won't get in the way."

Cal and Daniel exchanged a look and then Cal sighed, as if to say *"What do we have to lose now?"*

Anna knew he didn't trust her, but Daniel did, and that's all that mattered.

"Okay, what did you have in mind?" Daniel asked.

* * *

CAL WAS SURPRISED to realize that he agreed with everything Anna said. He was usually the one giving commands. Even when it came to Daniel, the choice almost always kicked back to Cal. Now here was this young woman, who was bright to be sure, offering them assistance, not the other way around. It was a good plan, well thought out, despite having almost no time to think about it. Cal was impressed, both at Anna's analytical mind and the fact that Diane had been quick to jump to her defense. With that in mind, and Daniel also standing next to Anna, Cal said, "Okay, Anna. Make the call."

Anna slid a phone from her purse, dialed a number and spoke quickly in Russian. It took no longer than twenty seconds when Anna looked up and said, "We're all set. They'll be here in five minutes."

Cal was doubly impressed. When they had the luxury of

time, Cal would have to ask Anna about her resources. Maybe they could share. But now was not the time. Cal had that creeping feeling that things were about to start moving very fast, like the billowing winds of battle now swirling into a tempest.

Then, as if fulfilling some unspoken prophesy, he heard Liberty growl, her body ramrod straight, nose pointed straight at the door. Cal and Daniel were moving at the same time, each grabbing one of the women and pulling them to cover.

Not a split second later, the lights went out. With a loud blast, the door crashed in, the dim lighting from the hallway illumined the five forms bursting into the room. Then everything happened at once.

Liberty let out a stream of barks turning the men's attention to her. It gave Cal and Daniel just the distraction they needed. They both leapt over the bed and into the fray. As if on cue, Liberty jumped onto the mass of bodies as well. That's when Cal felt, rather than heard, the first bullet and then another blow past him.

Cal tuned it all out and focused on the task at hand. Soon chaos reigned and the battle was full on.

CHAPTER THIRTEEN

Rourke screamed into the microphone, but it was too late. He'd heard the sounds. He'd heard when the bastard, a French subcontractor that Rourke had hired, gave the order to rush the room.

Rourke had sent them in to get Anna out quietly. He couldn't have her mixed up in this mess. His orders had been explicit, but the rogue contractor had gone off script. He'd been a cowboy with all the swagger of John Wayne, from the moment they'd touched down.

Rourke hired him because the man was good. His surveillance techniques were flawless, but now he'd put the operation at risk. He'd put Anna at risk; for that Rourke promised himself the man would pay.

Rourke listened to the scuffle as he watched the street. He chastised himself for not having them wear video cameras, at least then he could better understand what was going on, but there had been no time.

He pulled the surveillance team, told them to get changed and go in and snatch Anna. He flinched once when he heard the gunshots over the radio, and then again when the window blew. The police would be coming soon, and while Rourke had a good relationship with the local authorities, it was impossible for anyone to ignore gunshots in the middle of Paris.

He did the only thing he could, he threw everything into a backpack while still holding his hand cupped over his left ear so he could hear what was going on across the street.

Something had happened to the radio. Rourke tore it from his ear and shoved it in the backpack while he broke into a sprint for the door. He headed down the dimly lit corridor and ran bursting through the door at the end of the hall leaping first down to the first landing, then to the next.

He thought he heard distant sirens, but he couldn't be sure. It could just be the ringing in his ears, the blood coursing through his pounding heart.

He somehow skidded to a halt on the slick stone floor, took a quick breath in and then out, then eased the door to the street open. Yes, there was the sound of multiple sirens – definitely more than one.

Rourke wouldn't be surprised to see a military convoy rolling down the street at any moment. The city was on high alert for terrorist attacks. It was nothing like his first visit to Paris twenty years prior.

Parisians always had that laissez-faire attitude and went with the flow. Hell, they'd been through a Nazi occupation. Now, it was impossible not to notice heightened awareness, a symptom of their collective new reality.

Rourke was about to ease the door further open when there was a commotion across the street followed by the squeal of tires. He glanced right first and saw four black SUVs tearing down the narrow street, side-swiping the mirror of a parked car.

Four forms emerged from the hotel. No, make that five; the dog was with them too.

Rourke's eyes found Anna, and his stomach twisted when he saw she was being helped along by Daniel Briggs. She was limping.

Rourke couldn't tell in the dim light if there was blood dripping from her form. She looked disheveled, but none the worse for the wear, and then the Range Rovers screeched to a halt. Anna pointed to the one in the middle.

She limped over to it quickly, and then for some inexplicable reason, she looked across the hood to where he was hiding, watching them, and for that briefest moment, their eyes met.

Rourke slid back further into the doorway, but now she was gone. The powerful engines were steering the convoy down the street.

How could she have seen him? When Rourke replayed that moment in his head, he was surprised to find that her eyes hadn't gone wide, but instead they'd narrowed. With that realization, he realized that things had taken a turn, and fate would soon drag him from his intended path.

CHAPTER FOURTEEN

D iane breathed in and out, trying to calm her body. Once her fight-or-flight response had kicked into high gear, she hadn't seen much of what had happened in the room, but she'd felt it. When she stepped back and tried to analyze the situation, all she could feel was the blood pumping in her ears.

The only thing she could compare it to was the time she'd been mugged in Venice. It had been quick and non-violent, but she still remembered the intense fear that bodily harm might befall her.

She'd been a child then, barely nineteen, the lucky one in her Navy command who'd gotten time to take leave. So, she toured Italy, thinking it would be the perfect chance. Venice had been her first and last stop. She returned to her detachment shaken, and she never told a soul about it.

But now, as the line of Range Rovers tore down the Champs-Elysées, she felt like that nineteen-year-old again, her body unwilling to move to her command.

When she finally settled her breathing, she took it all in. Cal was sitting next to her, but he wasn't doing anything to soothe her. He was looking all around, trying to pinpoint any potential risk.

Then there was Daniel. You wouldn't have known that he had just been in a life-or-death struggle. He was as calm as could be, occasionally glancing out the window. The only emotion he showed was the fact that he had his hand on top of Anna's.

It had all happened so quickly that Diane still couldn't put the pieces together. There had been the break-in and then the rush of bodies. She remembered Cal and Daniel going up and over the bed, two men against five. There were gunshots and a violent struggle.

Punches never found a waiting person like they did in the movies. It sounded like a rubber mallet hitting the ground, not the wet slaps of Jackie Chan and Bruce Lee, and then it was over.

The gunshots had been shocking, but no one had been hit. The two women had been dragged through the room by Cal and Daniel. Diane thought she remembered Anna falling and Daniel scooping her up under his arm.

It was all such a blur, why couldn't she focus? It was Liberty nuzzling her hand that brought Diane back. She looked down at the dog's brown eyes staring up at her, wide, as if asking if she were okay.

"I'm okay." Diane whispered to the dog. Liberty licked her palm in response. Diane almost jumped, her hands protectively over Liberty, when Cal pointed ahead and said to the driver, "There, stop there."

Diane craned her neck to try to see what Cal was talking about, but she couldn't see past the muscle-bound driver. "We should get out of the city," Anna said.

"We will," Daniel replied for Cal, "I think I know what Cal has in mind."

With Cal in the back seat, Diane had felt like she was all

alone. He hadn't said a word to her. His mind was focused on the mission. Daniel and Anna seemed to be in their own little world, so it was just Diane and Liberty.

Diane shivered. She was cold now so she held onto the dog like a lifeline, needing the warmth as much as her presence. Liberty must have sensed that because when the Range Rover stopped and the side doors flew open, Liberty waited for Diane instead of bolting out like she usually did.

It was only then that Diane realized, as she slipped from the car, that the streets were still packed with pedestrians. It felt like an entire night had passed, but in reality, it had just started for the popular downtown.

She saw Cal walking towards a line of cars on the side street. They were all high-end sports cars, and while Diane didn't know, she was pretty sure they were Lamborghinis and Ferraris. There was a lime green one, a sleek black one in the middle, and a cherry-red one in the back.

Tourists were gathered around the cars, taking pictures as if they themselves owned the impressive vehicles. Cal went straight for a Middle Eastern looking young man in a red shirt.

Diane's senses were coming back now. She remembered seeing similar displays earlier in the day. Cars with signs on them. "Eighty Euros, Rent for fifteen minutes." They'd observed a race between two Chinese friends as they zoomed by around lunch time.

Cal was back now. "Everyone get in the red one," Cal ordered. Daniel ushered them that way.

"No, no dog," said the employee in the red shirt, pointing to Liberty. Cal didn't say a word, just slipped the man a couple of bills and that shut him up.

Cal got in the driver's seat, the company rep on the passenger side and somehow Daniel, Anna, Diane and

Liberty squeezed in the back. Diane barely had her seat buckled when Cal revved the engine and they were off.

The sports car salesman was attempting to regale them with all the fine virtues of his charge, but no one was listening. Cal's eyes were locked ahead. Diane's eyes went wide when she saw where Cal was going, straight into oncoming traffic. Their host pointed and said, "Monsieur, careful!" Still Cal ignored him, and at the very last possible second, he swerved to the left and darted down a back alley.

Over the ancient cobblestones they went, the car's shocks doing the best they could to keep the passengers comfortable. There was a torque and grind. Twice Diane thought that Liberty would fly from her arms, but they made it out the other side.

Cal scanned the streets and then said over his shoulder "Do you see anything?"

Diane thought he was talking to her, but then Daniel answered, "I think we're clear."

By now their host was shaken. Diane wasn't sure if it was so much the ride, but the demeanor of the driver, but he said "Monsieur, if you stop the car, I will refund half your money." Cal ignored him and pulled into traffic, this time more carefully.

They weaved in and out slowly, going with the flow, passing a tour bus, a double-decker loaded with tourists and then a young family of three jammed onto a Moped. He stomped on the gas and they swerved around an inky black Rolls Royce, its driver not even looking up in surprise.

"We've got at least two behind us," Daniel announced. Cal cut across traffic, then darted down another side street, the car narrowly missing a grocery-laden pedestrian.

"Which way to the airport?" Cal asked their host.

The man was visibly upset. When he answered, his lips quivered, "Take a left there," the man said, pointing up ahead.

Cal did as instructed and soon they were free of the traffic. "The airport is too far," their host said in protest, "I will get in trouble."

In response, Cal pulled over to the side of the road. "Get out," he said to the host. The man's face colored, and Diane thought she saw him reach into his coat.

Daniel grabbed him by the back of the neck, and then reached around the man and came back out holding a sheathed knife. "Do you have a card?" Daniel asked him.

"What?" he replied.

"I said, do you have a card?" The man was completely unnerved. "A business card with your phone number on it," Daniel explained.

The man nodded, his face ashen, and then reached into his pocket slowly, producing a gold business card holder. Daniel snatched it and extracted one of the cards. "We'll call you and let you know exactly where it's parked, I promise." It was obvious the man wasn't convinced because he clutched the armrest like it would take a hundred men to pry him from it.

"Get out," Cal said again, playing bad cop to Daniel's good.

The man actually looked back at Anna and Diane, but if he was looking for sympathy, he was looking in the wrong place. After seeing he wasn't going to get any help, he exhaled and opened the door. Daniel gently helped him on his way, patted him on the back and then took the man's seat.

"Please be careful, I..." Diane couldn't hear what the man finished saying, because Cal had already rocketed away from the sidewalk, leaving the man open-mouthed, no doubt thinking that he would never see the red convertible again.

CHAPTER FIFTEEN

"Tell me exactly what happened!" Ian Rourke barked at his team leader. He'd just gotten word that one of his marks had disappeared, somehow eluding his men on the busy streets of Paris.

Rourke's team leader explained how Cal and his companions had vacated the black Range Rovers and piled in one of those high-end rentals that now clogged the side streets of the Champs-Elysées.

Rourke silently chided himself for not having more pursuit vehicles on hand. By the time the five men who had gone into the hotel emerged, a fleeing Cal Stokes was long gone. Rourke glared at the five men as he listened to the team leader on the phone.

"Okay, find out who owns that car and find out if they have a GPS tracker on it. It will turn up somewhere," Rourke ended the call. His pursuit team knew what to do; they'd done it a hundred times.

It would be a painstaking process and probably fruitless. He was beginning to see how easily Stokes and Briggs could slip out of the tightest nets, but Rourke wouldn't give up that quickly. Even the smartest men made the dumbest decisions sometimes.

Now he had to deal with the five who had come back to the safe house, bloodied and bedraggled. Four of them looked somewhat contrite. They knew what had happened. They'd been bested even with the odds in their favor; it had been five against two. Rourke didn't count the girlfriend and Anna. However, one of his men had returned with one pants leg torn and a nasty gash on his calf, courtesy of Stokes's dog.

It was the man who had taken the lead that Rourke focused on now. He was a Frenchman known simply as Maurice. There was no contrition on the man's face, even as he dabbed a towel on his split lip, and he sported what was sure to become an impressive black eye.

"I told you to wait for my order," Rourke said to him.

"There was no time," Maurice said. "The manager said that they had cars coming, that they had possibly called for taxis. I couldn't take the chance."

"We couldn't take the chance," Rourke said slowly.

"Eh? Oh, yes, we we. Ha, ha! That's funny! Oui, oui," Maurice chuckled.

Rourke was on the man in a flash, grabbing him by the back of his greasy head, yanking him back so hard his Adam's apple was exposed. That was where Rourke clamped down his other hand.

Maurice looked right back at Rourke, completely undaunted.

The other men were watching now with great interest. It was rare that their boss lost his temper. He had a reputation for swift action if needed, but 9.9 times out of ten, the situation dictated a calm and steady hand.

Rourke thought of Anna. He knew he might kill this man.

"There were civilians in that room," Rourke growled, "and who the hell told you to take a live weapon in with you?" His orders had been clear, Tasers and dart guns only. "Do you know what the French authorities would do if they had caught you?"

Still no response from Maurice. The man truly didn't care. But then that last glimpse of Anna flashed in Rourke's mind, and instead of lashing out with his words, Rourke's head slammed down, his forehead connecting solidly with the man's oversized nose. Rourke felt a crunch, and he pushed the man away.

Maurice stumbled back, holding his nose. There were tears in his eyes, an involuntary reflex. He then dabbed at his nose with the same wet towel he'd been holding moments before.

"You should not have done that," Maurice said evenly, "My superiors will hear of this." The Frenchman left without saying another word.

The other four, all Americans, looked to Rourke for orders as if they expected to be told to bring Maurice back, but no order came.

Rourke's frustration had played out. Maurice wouldn't soon forget. A man like that had his uses, and Rourke knew the type. The Frenchman wouldn't go tattling to his local boss. He would figure out another way to get even.

Rourke didn't care. The man was of no consequence, just a hired thug brought in to do a job, and now that job was over.

Or at least, Rourke thought, there was no way that Stokes would stay in Paris. They would try to first get out of the city and then out of the country. Their final destination would have to be America, but that could be a challenge to reach directly.

He was sure that a few phone calls could put his query on the radar of Homeland Security, effectively shutting them out of the country, but then that might affect Anna, Rourke mused. He was uncomfortable with this feeling. Indecision had never been one of his weaknesses, and yet now, he felt his judgment clouding.

There was more at stake now if the government was involved. That meant the FBI and possibly other internal agencies would be alerted as to what was happening. The best thing to do was to remove Anna from the picture and get her to safety. Then Rourke and his team could do their jobs.

Either way, Congressman McKnight needed an update. At that moment, Rourke decided that he would tell the Congressman about the botched snatch job, but that they were in hot pursuit of Stokes and Briggs.

His men in Vienna already had three of the others, and the two Jefferson Group men in Amsterdam would turn up eventually.

Really, the damage had already been done. The Jefferson Group was effectively out of commission, and on the laptop on the corner desk of the room was all the information McKnight would need to connect the president with the men of The Jefferson Group.

McKnight didn't know that Rourke had the information yet. The experienced security man knew it was best to hold such information until the end of the job. It was always advisable to tie up loose threads before presenting the coup de grâce.

And yet, as Rourke absently gave the four remaining men their orders, he thought about what it might mean to release the treasured information. He would have to think on that: its effects on America, but more importantly, the implications for Anna Varushkin.

CHAPTER SIXTEEN

"Thank you, Mr. President. I'll see you in a couple days." Congressman McKnight shook the hand of the President of the United States.

"I'll try to go easy on you," Brandon Zimmer said with a smile.

McKnight nodded and left the Oval Office. He didn't want to leave. He knew it was where he belonged.

McKnight and the president did make it a habit to check in with one another during the campaign. As far as Zimmer knew, they were friends. When word had leaked out to the media that the two newfound rivals still kept up their old routine despite the upcoming debates and election, some outlets touted it as a new era in American politics. Like Ronald Reagan and Tip O'Neil of the twentieth century, when political rivals worked together for the well-being of their country.

If they only knew the truth.

The entire time he'd been talking to President Zimmer, he was thinking about two things. First, what he would do to redecorate the Oval Office. Second, what Zimmer's face would look like when his world came crashing down. That made it easier to smile and nod, and go along with the president's idle chit-chat.

There were so many other things to do, but McKnight had to keep up appearances. The good news had come in late the night before. Rourke had struck gold. They'd infiltrated The Jefferson Group's network. Rourke himself was now in possession of information that would damage the sitting president.

McKnight needed that boost now. The excitement and confidence from the Republican National Convention was gone. He'd faced reality. The true and tested President Brandon Zimmer was the heavy favorite, garnering almost sixty percent of the presumptive vote. Research had shown that McKnight and Zimmer were just too much alike, and that America for the most part was happy with the way things were being run. That made McKnight anything but happy.

While he smiled and waved at rallies across the country, he secretly seethed. Sure, people voted along party lines, but the left had seen a resurgence with Zimmer in power. The president had somehow done the impossible in a world where private interests and lobbies ruled the day. Zimmer had somehow stayed above the fray. Sure, he leaned more conservative for some things, and more liberal for others. However, McKnight had to admit that Zimmer had crafted a well-rounded administration and that his policies were almost entirely in line with McKnight's own.

McKnight grinned when he realized soon that wouldn't matter. His hunch had been right. His sixth sense had always served him well. While other politicians might zig, McKnight liked to zag.

The question now was when to release the information. It needed to be done when it would be most damaging to the president, and when McKnight would be in the best position to pick up the pieces and scatter the burning wreckage into the ocean. For now, only he and Rourke knew the breadth of the operation.

McKnight felt very much like the experienced Zen master, quietly sowing seeds that he would soon harvest. There had always been the concern that Rourke might talk, but after further consultation with the head of the Republican National Committee, McKnight felt that such a leak would never happen. Besides, if Rourke ever wavered, there were ways of dealing with him.

For now, McKnight needed the information that Rourke had. Proof that not only was the president in league with private mercenaries, but also that he was funneling American money and resources into their pockets. Once the internet got hold of that, well, the story would be spun in a thousand different directions. Each tale would grow more twisted than the last.

President Brandon Zimmer, a shining example of what an American president should be, would then be compared to Russian government leaders in league with the Russian mob.

Then more pointed questions would arise. How many more operations had the president ordered that were off the books? It made McKnight want to do a little dance right there in the White House hallway. Instead, he grinned at a pretty White House intern, who smiled shyly back. "Have a wonderful day," McKnight said. The girl's lips moved, but no words came out. Her face reddened and McKnight waved his goodbye. The girl better start packing her things. The president's fifteen minutes in the spotlight was coming to an end.

In his place, would step The Matador, Florida's Congressman, Antonio McKnight. The new face of the Republican Party. A man of the people and for the people, a man who'd come from nothing. He'd escaped the ravages of a broken home, yet somehow managed to climb tooth and nail above the masses. The new shining beacon for the world to see. *Yes,* McKnight thought, *what had once been a dream is now becoming reality.*

As he was escorted to his own mini-motorcade, McKnight allowed the warm feeling to wash over him like a bath in the fountain of youth. McKnight sat back and closed his eyes as the motorcade sped off. It wouldn't be long now and he would have a new home.

CHAPTER SEVENTEEN

Lydia set the teacup in the jumble of dishes in the sink. She really should wash them, but she was tired. It had been a long day at the café, capped off by a group of drunken tourists that just couldn't take the hint that it was time to leave. So, after ushering them out and helping the rest of the staff clean up, Lydia walked home alone, tired, relishing the feel of her bed.

But when she'd gotten to her small flat, she was wide awake again. It was one of the penalties for working so late. You got used to the hours; when small things happened you just couldn't stop your mind from wandering. So, she made a cup of tea and replayed the day.

She thought about writing in her journal, an old habit picked up from her father. However, when her mind was spinning she couldn't focus enough to sit and write. Besides, Lydia wasn't one to write about trivialities. The journal was about concrete experiences, things she one day hoped to put in a book.

Her father, a former college professor, had encouraged her and gave her the journal years before on a trip to Croatia.

Since that time, Lydia had seen much of the world. Because her mother had died when Lydia was only a child, she and her father had taken trains across Europe, ships across the Mediterranean Sea and airplanes to Australia and China.

Now her father was retired. He spent his days volunteering at the Van Gogh Museum, shooing naughty children away from touching paintings, or scolding shutter-happy tourists who just couldn't get the point that no pictures meant no pictures. However, he was kind with his warnings, using the same warm smile he'd given Lydia countless times over her lifetime.

Her thoughts shifted back to the unexpected surprise awaiting her as she had begun her shift - Willy Trent. Lydia smiled as she said the name in her mind. One of Lydia's gifts in life allowed her to interact with wonderful people and she would "collect" delightful memories of them, almost like gathering shells from the beach or taking photos of stunning sunsets. It was one of the amazing things about traveling. You met all sorts of characters. Whether old or young, it didn't matter; each one had their own story.

But in Lydia's eyes, to find a truly whole person who lived with an open heart was a rare find. She had been utterly surprised to find that quality in an American, of all people. He was a black, seven-foot-tall, military man who really knew what it meant to live. Not only that, he was smart in a way that Lydia could relate to. He was like a vacuum soaking up bits of life and recalling them whenever he needed them, whether to brighten a friend's day or to tell a bawdy joke.

They'd been friends from the start. It was impossible not to love Willy, and maybe if things had been different, there could have been something more. But the timing had never worked out, and, to be fair, Willy had never groused. He was a gentleman.

He always respected her space, always inquired of her

latest boyfriend, of which there had been a few. But when he showed up earlier in the day with his friend, Lydia couldn't help but open her own heart. It wasn't an uncomfortable feeling, but for some reason it made Lydia sad. It was the fact that she didn't know exactly what Willy did for a living. She couldn't put the pieces together.

At last, she slipped into her pajamas and got ready for bed. She did her best to forget about Willy. He was gone, after all. He'd said it was just a quick visit—his first vacation in ages. Part of Lydia had wanted to pack her bags and join him on the adventure, but she wasn't that forward. She was just about to turn off the lights when she heard a knock at the door.

Her hand froze over the light switch. It was almost three in the morning; who could be calling? Lydia padded her way to the front door and grabbed a fire poker by the fireplace as she passed. She'd been robbed twice while she'd been at work, so she was leery.

Instead of heading straight for the door, she went to one of the windows, eased the curtain aside just an inch. Lydia breathed a sigh of relief and she went for the door. When she opened it, the night presented her with quite the spectacle. There he was: Willy Trent with his friend Gaucho. They were both dripping wet.

"Willy, what happened?" she asked.

The two men exchanged a look, and then Willy grinned. "Well, it being Gaucho's first time in Amsterdam and all, he thought that maybe we should take a swim in the canals."

The comment was ridiculous of course, but Lydia knew it was Willy's way to avoid what had truly happened. Thus, she wouldn't ask any more questions about what had happened, unless he brought it up.

"Do you mind if we come in and get dried off?" Willy

asked, "We could take our things off out here and you can throw them in the dryer if that's okay."

"No, no, please come in. Don't worry about the floors." The two men walked in trailing the familiar scent of canal water, but they went no further than the entryway before they were stripping down to their underwear. Willy did it as if it were the most natural thing.

It was Gaucho who'd looked at her with just a hint of embarrassment. Lydia grabbed a laundry basket and took all the wet clothes to her tiny laundry nook to start the wash.

"Do you mind if we grab a quick shower?" Trent asked coming up behind her.

"I wish you would," Lydia said, "Are you sure you weren't swimming through the sewers?"

"It sure felt like it. Towels in the same place?" Lydia nodded, and Willy pointed at the bedroom door, allowing Gaucho to go first.

Ten minutes later, both men were showered and wearing Lydia's pink and purple towels around their waists, nursing beers at the kitchen counter.

"Are you sure you don't mind us staying here, Lydia? I don't want to be any trouble."

"It's fine Willy, as long as you guys don't mind sleeping on the couch and the floor."

"I call couch," Gaucho said like a child calling to be in the front seat of a car.

"I couldn't fit my body on that thing anyway." Willy said. "Lydia, we won't be able to sleep for a bit; you can head to bed if you like. We'll be quiet."

"No, it's fine, I'm not tired." Curiosity got the better of her and she asked, "Can you tell me what happened?"

Willy shrugged and took a long pull from his beer. "Not much to tell really. Got back to our hotel room and someone was in there. I chased him halfway across Amsterdam before he disappeared. You'd think he'd be hard to miss with his white track suit and all, but man, was that guy fast!"

"You've got that right!" Gaucho said, raising his beer, "I still can't believe the cops never showed up. Do they not do much around here? You'd think with all your cafés that they'd have their hands full." It was a common question.

"The natives don't give the police much trouble," Lydia said, "and the tourists, for the most part are respectful. I think the city officials would rather have you tourists high on marijuana than drunk on beer. I have seen that firsthand."

"Do you get a lot of troublemakers at work?"

Lydia shrugged, "Sometimes, but I can handle it. If you don't make trouble for them, most of them won't make trouble for you."

Lydia left out the fact that being a pretty girl in a room full of drunks wasn't always the most comfortable situation. Sometimes hands swarmed her and she would have to back away from them playfully. She had to make a living after all, but she didn't want to say anything like that in front of Willy, so she changed the subject. "That still doesn't explain what you were doing going for a midnight swim."

Again, that look between the two men, as if they were deciding whether to tell her the truth. "The guy in the white track suit wasn't alone," Willy said, "and they turned the tables on us. Pretty soon we were the ones on the run."

"On the run or on the swim?" Lydia asked with a smile.

Willy chuckled, "That was Gaucho's idea."

"Hey," Gaucho said in protest, "you said it was a good idea."

"I said it might be a good idea. But before I could give you any alternatives, you had to jump. It's just like you Army doggies taking a leap before you really think about things. You know you owe me a new phone, right?" Gaucho waved the comment away like it didn't matter.

"You can use my phone if you need to." Lydia offered.

"That's okay," Willy said, "I'll pick up a prepaid phone in the morning. Is that shop around the corner still there? The one run by the Egyptian guy?"

"Yes," Lydia said, "I can go down there now if you'd like." She offered.

"No, it can wait until morning."

"Are you sure? Maybe we should..." Gaucho started.

"No, it'll wait. Besides, probably better to lay low tonight anyway and pick it back up in the morning."

Lydia wondered why Willy did not want to use her phone. Then her mind made the leap. It was because he didn't want her to get tracked. She knew that now. What she also knew was that, no matter the danger, she would help him.

CHAPTER EIGHTEEN

The LED light flickered overhead each time Dr. Higgins nodded off. The box-shaped room was the most comfortable interrogation room Higgins had ever been in; it had actual leather armchairs in the corners of the room. Of course, they were of no use to Higgins because his wrists were shackled to the impressive oak table in the middle of the room. The first few hours he'd been there, he marveled at the grain of the wood, going row by row, comparing the colors. To keep his mind occupied, he first imagined the man who had cut down the tree and then he imagined the man who had crafted the table.

Higgins had always known that if he'd chosen to live a simple life, he would have done woodworking of some sort. It fit his meticulous nature with the high attention to detail. One blemish could ruin an entire project. Cut too short, and you had to find another piece. Cut too deep and your master-piece was ruined forever.

Maybe I will take up woodworking, Higgins thought. They were the idle thoughts of a man who had nothing but time.

He considered the plights of Neil and Jonas, of course.

They were probably in similar rooms, and he hoped they were well. Jonas could probably take care of himself. He might be counting on the authorities to get the American Consulate, not that it would help. Higgins had been through enough of these situations to know that this was not a Viennese-run operation. It had nothing to do with the fact that the driver of the police cruiser had been an American. It had everything to do with the man's demeanor. He wanted something, and he wouldn't stop until he got it.

The one who really worried Higgins was Neil. He'd been in a similar situation before. As a psychologist, Higgins wondered what the hours were doing to Neil's head, and how he was handling the psychological torture.

No doubt Neil's mind was reliving the time under Nick Ponder's cruel reign. In that ordeal, he'd lost his foot, just above the ankle. He'd been subjected to torture, extreme temperatures and, worst of all, despair.

Higgins had always marveled that loss of hope was what usually did men in. Promising death was easy. Ripping away hope was not. When they were stripped bare, when everything had been taken from them, when their captors carefully implanted the idea that the person under intense scrutiny had no options left, that everything was gone, that they were like an amoeba floating in nothingness; it truly frightened any reasonable man to the core.

That worried Higgins most about Neil Patel. Despite his scientific profession, Higgins found himself praying for his friend. *Do not lose hope, Neil. Do not give in to your fears. Do not let the demons win.*

Yet, it was impossible to be unafraid; the outcomes were unknown. Even he, a veteran of countless interrogations, albeit on the other side of the table, found it hard not to be afraid. Fear of the unknown crept in like a silent cat, waiting for that perfect moment to pounce.

Higgins looked around the room again. He didn't see any cameras, but he knew they were there. He thought they might have even rigged the light overhead to flicker whenever the subject began to fall asleep. It could just be in his mind, but to Higgins there were no coincidences. There had also been the time when he had actually nodded off and someone came barging into the room, only to set down a glass of water or a cup of coffee. The thought made Higgins's mind snap back into place.

They had taken his watch, and there was no clock on the wall, so he had no idea what time it was. There were no windows, another tactic to make subjects squirm. He knew that all it took was a feeling of claustrophobia for some to bend and break. He'd never had a problem with small spaces, but even Higgins could admit that after hours of just staring at walls, you could almost feel them closing in. So, he busied himself with thinking of Neil, wishing that his thoughts would stay positive. He thought of Jonas, and how he might use his considerable resources to have them released. Higgins thought of Cal and Daniel who'd stayed in Paris. Did they know what had happened?

Then Higgins laughed when he thought of MSgt. Willy and of Gaucho. They never seemed to do things the easy way, yet they always came out on top, grinning like boys who just pulled off the best prank in history at their high school.

He wondered if either Trent or Gaucho had gone through interrogation training. Gaucho undoubtedly had during his valiant time in Delta force. He knew that Marine pilots and Special Operations personnel went through SERE training, but everyday riflemen never got that chance.

Not that Higgins worried about Master Sergeant Willy Trent. He could take care of himself and it had nothing to do with the man's physique. It was all in Willy's psyche and his attitude. It had always fascinated Dr. Higgins the way warriors could be so different and yet the same. Trent was fierce when that was needed, but overwhelmingly kind, like a candy-dispensing grandfather: always happy, always smiling. What would Willy have done if he hadn't enlisted in the Marine Corps?

Higgins chided himself for letting his mind wander, another symptom of captivity. He'd studied it for years, decades even. He knew of the histories of men who'd spent years in a Hanoi prison. He'd even interviewed some. Then there were the hell holes like those in the Middle East, where they treated sinners like cattle to be slaughtered. Those interviews with former prisoners opened his eyes to another level of cruelty. Higgins shivered at the thought.

Higgins didn't think it was likely that that would happen here. The Viennese authorities might go along with whatever operation this was because it undoubtedly had the stamp of someone's approval: an official request. However, the Austrians were civilized people, they wouldn't let torture happen under their watch. Not in Vienna.

Higgins was almost ashamed that that realization made him relax. Should he have wanted the pain? The challenge somehow allowed him to clinically detach his mind from his own body and watch to see if he could take the strain. He'd gone through pain in role playing and training, of course, but when you were actually in that potential seat of torture, your body ached. When your mind flipped and flopped with exhaustion and panic, it was easy to see how men and women could say things that weren't the truth. Because wasn't the truth what was needed? Isn't that what every interrogator wanted?

No. You're telling yourself a story again. Higgins thought to himself. *You're tired. Close your eyes, rest. It won't matter. They won't hurt you. You'll get out of this soon.*

So Higgins closed his eyes. He welcomed the darkness.

"Sleep," he commanded himself. Somewhere he felt his chin hit his chest but just as quickly, the interrogation room door slammed open and a nondescript man walked in with a paper cup, set it down in front of Dr. Higgins and left.

The prisoner looked down. More water. Higgins snorted then, but before picking up the cup he realized he had to use the restroom. "One point in your favor," Higgins said and then pulled his hands back, clasped them together and waited.

CHAPTER NINETEEN

C al watched the homeless man shuffle by wearing soiled hospital scrubs like he had just been released from a mental asylum. His feet were covered in gray duct tape, but the gray could only be seen along the top of his foot. The rest of it was black from use. Other than the way he looked, face dark with filth, the man looked like he was out for a morning stroll to get his cup of coffee and a newspaper. No one gave him a second glance.

The train station was mostly empty anyway. The vendors were just starting to show up and the light on the ticket booths turned on. The homeless man wandered over to a public piano in the middle of the station. He sat down, ran a hand across the keyboard. Cal wondered if it might be one of those hidden camera scenarios that you see on social media when a famous musician shows up in the middle of Times Square and amazes the masses. But instead of Beethoven or even Chopsticks, the man just started pounding on the keyboard, sending discordant music into the air. Now Cal looked at him more because of the tainted melody and not due to actual annoyance.

Cal put the man out of his head and kept scanning around. They had ditched the Ferrari miles away and had taken a succession of cabs back into the city. The five of them had spent a good hour just walking without much being said. Even Daniel looked and acted more morose than usual. No, not morose—brooding. Liberty was simply content to be with Master and their friends; them resting on a park bench, her curled up safely next to them.

Without their luggage, they had picked up a few items along the way. Cal wore a baseball cap of some soccer team he didn't know, along with a coat that Diane had bargained down to almost half the listed price. Diane had taken it all in stride. Anna just looked happy to be with Daniel.

So strange, Cal thought. Their room had just been busted into. They'd been attacked. Now they were on the run. And yet, here Daniel and Anna sat, two content friends who were probably growing to be more than that.

Cal switched back to business.

It was too dangerous to use credit cards or even phones, so they were without the most basic of resources until Anna had announced she would be more than happy to finance their journey. Cal almost chimed in with a "We'll pay you back," before he remembered that Anna could probably afford it. Neither Daniel nor Anna had said anything about it, but you could just tell with somebody like Anna about what her life now was. She no longer wanted for any material thing.

"Oh, do you smell that?" Diane said excitedly.

"Coffee!" Anna answered for her.

"Mmmm, let's go get some. Do you boys want a cup?" Diane asked.

"Please," Cal said.

"Make that two," Daniel said.

The girls stood up from the bench and walked off, Anna holding Diane's arm. The two women looking quite European in their manner. When they were out of ear shot, Cal asked his friend, "You think Amsterdam's the best way to go? I don't like that we haven't heard from Top and Gaucho. It's not that they can't take care of themselves, but there is safety in numbers, you know?"

Daniel nodded. He said he had been thinking the same thing when the idea of heading to Amsterdam had hit him. There was always the chance that their friends might be coming this way, but that couldn't be avoided. Paris wasn't safe, at least not for Cal's merry band of intrepid runaways. "And you still think it's a good idea to take a train instead of renting a car or taking a bus?" Cal asked. It had been Daniel's idea to take the train.

"It's the fastest way," Daniel said. "I don't know why, but I think we need to get there very quick."

"Too bad there wasn't an earlier train," Cal mused. Liberty looked up from the ground where she was lying as a train pulled into the station, hissing as it came to a stop. Satisfied that it presented no danger, the dog put her head back down on her paws and closed her eyes. *Oh, to be a dog*, Cal thought, *Life sure would be easier*.

The girls returned, handing the men cups of steaming coffee. Cal took his gratefully, thanking Anna, their current benefactor. She smiled and then cocked her head. "I wasn't sure I should tell you this, and I don't think it makes any difference, but I think I saw something."

"Where? Here?" Daniel asked.

"No, back at the hotel when we were leaving. I can't be sure, but there was someone across the street in the doorway."

"What did he look like?" Cal asked.

"He looked familiar," Anna said, blowing on her coffee. "It was just a moment, and I couldn't be for sure, but I could have sworn I knew the man. It was dark, and most of his face was covered in shadow, but there was something there. I don't know. It might be nothing."

Cal chuckled, "It seems to be the only nothing we have to go on right now, so keep thinking about it, okay? Tell us if you remember." Anna nodded and sipped her coffee. *It could be nothing,* Cal told himself, but Anna was anything but stupid. She wouldn't have brought it up unless she truly believed it was important.

Maybe there was a connection and maybe there wasn't. There was no way of going back now to find out, but at least it was something, and in Cal's current state of mind, something was better than nothing. At this moment, it was better to stew on the mysterious face in the shadows than to worry about his friends.

He would have given anything to be able to pick up a phone to call Top or Gaucho to make sure they were okay. Sure, he was worried about his own safety, but he was more concerned about Diane. He never really worried about Daniel, but focused his concern on the others: Dr. Higgins, Neil, and Jonas. Jonas was a civilian. Had he gotten caught up in this, too?

And then there was The Jefferson Group. What was Brandon thinking? His most effective secret asset had gone down; something Cal had promised would never happen. Not that anyone could give 100% assurances, but he thought they had been careful. The proof was in their current situation. They had not been careful enough. Now they were all in danger. Cal focused on the questions that had been nagging at him ever since Neil had alerted them about the security breach.

Who was behind it all? What where they after?

CHAPTER TWENTY

While Jonas Layton had never been in this kind of predicament before, he'd been under pressure plenty of times. You didn't get to be one of the youngest self-made billionaires in the world without going through trying times, countless late nights worrying about the launch of a product or whether he could make payroll the next day. His intuition and hard work had always paid off. He learned that triumphs racked up like mini trophies and that as time went on, the stress became more manageable, the hurdles only knee high. But now sitting in an interrogation room in Vienna, Austria, Jonas was beginning to doubt himself.

His path to The Jefferson Group had been anything but routine. When it really came down to it, he'd been bored. He'd conquered his world and was looking for more, something many of his old friends never understood. It didn't matter how much money you had, fifty bucks in the bank or fifty million. Life was still life. Without challenges there was no life, so while his buddies from high school and college envied him and imagined him sitting on some sun-soaked beach surrounded by half naked girls, that was far from his reality.

Take this trip to Europe, for example. It was his first real vacation in years. Sure, they were in Vienna to do a little bit of work. But talking to a bunch of people, students no less, about how to better themselves as well as provide them insights on what the "real world" was honestly like, didn't feel like work for Jonas. He truly enjoyed it and could have done it in his sleep.

Sleep. Jonas could use some sleep. They were watching him and Dr. Higgins a few rooms over. He knew because their timing was too perfect, politely coming into the room with a glass of water. At first he drank it thinking he should stay hydrated. Then his bladder filled, and he regretted the decision. He'd made some demands early on, but it seemed to Jonas that they'd been ignored.

Now he thought back again as to why he'd come to The Jefferson Group. Beyond the boredom and beyond the search to do something that actually mattered, Jonas had been lonely. So, when Cal Stokes, Daniel Briggs, Neil Patel, and Dr. Higgins had come into his life, not to mention Willy Trent and Gaucho, Jonas had felt the thrill of being let into a private club that few dared enter. Sure, there were risks, but they had the protection of Jonas's money and the President of the United States.

Jonas chuckled when he realized neither of those things mattered now. If someone wanted to arrest you and put you in a cell, they would do it. Billions be damned.

He worried that somehow Brandon Zimmer was catching the worst of it. That was what concerned Jonas most. He was concerned not with his own wellbeing but the wellbeing of his friends. The men at The Jefferson Group had become his family.

Sure, Jonas had his own family, a mother and father who

were as bland as oatmeal, and they didn't really understand what Jonas did for a living. They still lived in the same three-bedroom house with the same pictures of Jonas in his youth soccer teams hanging on the wall. Jonas wondered what they would think if they knew he was sitting in a jail cell. Not that where he was sitting was anything like a real jail cell, but he figured his mom would still freak out. His dad would jump to conclusions before really knowing the facts.

That was the Layton family: Never make waves and never show your dark side. Jonas made it a point to see them only on holidays. You would think that as an only child he might see them more often, but whenever he visited, he felt less and less welcome. They were both retired now, not because of his money but solely on their own. His mother had been a school teacher, his father an accountant. They penny pinched for decades and now lived a comfortable retirement playing golf in the mornings when the weather allowed and sitting on the porch reading books until it was time for dinner.

Jonas shook his head. His mind was wandering now, and not for the first time he thought about how he'd escaped. He wondered why he was so different than both of his vanilla-flavored, totally bland parents. They were the heart of America - what made it beat, what made it go on. They represented Main Street, USA. And he was fluorescent orange, taking on challenges, one at a time.

Yeah, Mom would freak out if she saw me here now, he thought, laughing to himself again. He wondered how long it took to go crazy when you were sitting in solitary.

Then the door burst open and Jonas flinched involuntarily, even though he knew about and expected the comings and goings of the guards. It still rattled him. But when he looked up, it wasn't just the stern face of a guard coming in. There was also a familiar face.

"My God. Max!" Jonas said.

"Jonas, don't say a word." The man wore an impeccably tailored navy blue suit, his gleaming teeth caught the light when he snapped at the guard, "Undo those cuffs and find his friends. We're leaving in two minutes."

Jonas felt ashamed at the level of relief coursing through his veins as the handcuffs were undone from his wrists. He rose on shaky legs to face his old friend to say something.

"But, Max...."

Max put a finger to his lips for silence. "Where are his things?"

The guard avoided Max's eyes, nothing was gathered or offered.

"I said two minutes. Not a moment longer."

"Yes, sir," the guard said, leading them down the hall quickly now.

Jonas sidled up close to his friend and whispered, "Max, I need to go to the bathroom."

"Where is your restroom?" Max barked.

"But I thought you said... "

"I asked where the restroom is!"

The guard made a quick U-turn and soon they were at the bathroom, which was more of a locker room for the police officers.

Jonas wasn't the only one in there. Two more familiar faces looked over to him from the urinals. Dr. Higgins only nodded, but Neil looked up and said, "Jonas, what's going on?"

"I don't know, but let's not talk about it until we get out of here."

After finishing their business, they left, meeting Max in the hallway, who apparently stood guard like an alert Doberman.

"Where are their things?" he asked the guard.

"At the front desk. They're waiting, sir."

"Very well. Carry on."

They marched past both plainclothes and uniform clad police officers who did nothing to stifle their curiosity. Jonas knew it wasn't them. No one knew who the three men from America really were, but they knew who the unexpected visitor was. Everyone in Austria knew of Max Frazier. As they left through the front door, the eyes followed them. Jonas had no doubt that when the doors closed, the raucous chatter would begin.

* * *

NO ONE SAID a word as they climbed into the forest green Bentley, sunshine glinting off its perfectly polished wheels. Max got in the driver's seat and it wasn't until they left the police station behind them that his serious façade finally dropped.

"Were any of you mistreated?" he asked.

Everyone shook their heads. The adrenalin of their escape was finally wearing off. Dr. Higgins, more than the others, recognized the drop of adrenalin, but he had been expecting this. Even so, he found himself suddenly, exhaustingly tired. And yet, he was curious about the stranger. He had the air of nobility, and he had marched in like Napoleon himself, although the man behind the wheel of the Bentley stood at least an inch or two over six feet.

"Jonas, aren't you going to introduce us?" Higgins asked.

"Right, sorry. Neil Patel, Alan Higgins, this is my good friend, Maximilian Frazier."

"I hope you don't mind, but I'll shake your hands once we get a chance to stop. I'd like to put as much distance between us and your friends as possible."

It took moments for Higgins to realize what their benefactor was actually saying.

"We're being followed," Higgins guessed.

Frazier nodded. "Two cars. They're trying very hard to avoid being seen. One of the beauties of Vienna is the presence of so many one-way streets. But don't worry. There's a checkpoint up ahead, and I have way more horses under my hood than they do in their puny vehicles."

Sure enough, after a cursory examination, and after not one but two solicitations for autographs from the checkpoint guards, the Bentley was allowed through, and Maximilian Frazier gunned the engine, quickly putting anyone intent on the chase eating dust.

Once five minutes had gone by and everyone had relaxed, curiosity got the better of Higgins and he asked, "Jonas, the suspense is killing me. Would you please explain who this kind gentleman is and how we might repay him for his kindness? Oh, and an explanation of his celebrity would be appreciated as well."

Both Frazier and Jonas chuckled. "Would you like to do the honors?" Jonas asked his friend.

The driver shook his head. "Oh, no. I want to hear how you describe our first encounter."

They both laughed at the memory, and then Jonas began.

"If you hadn't guessed, Max is an old friend. Before he became a celebrity in his native Austria, he was just a lowly prince trying to find his way in the world. Of course, I had no idea about his background when we met. I had taken a semester off school to 'find myself' and thought it would be a good idea to backpack through Europe. Off I went with a few hundred dollars in my pocket. I made it through London all right and to Vienna. No, not to Vienna. To Rome. And don't you know, the first coffee shop I went into to get an espresso, all my money was taken. I didn't have a lira left, but luckily Max here saw the whole thing. He somehow pried himself away from the group of girls in the corner of the café, and came over to see if he could be of assistance."

"Oh, please, let me tell this part," Max said with a smile. Jonas nodded. "Jonas really tried to explain that nothing had happened, that he would be okay. I couldn't tell if he was too embarrassed or too proud to admit that he'd just been robbed, but I'd seen it happen many times before. I offered to buy his espresso, and then when it was obvious that a conversation with our friend Jonas here was much more illuminating than those forgettable young women..."

"Forgettable?" Jonas snorted.

Maximilian Frazier shrugged. "Espresso led to dinner, and then for the next week, Jonas stayed with me at my little place in Rome."

"Little place in Rome," Jonas said mockingly. "Let me tell you about Max's little place in Rome. It takes up the entire top floor of a building a stone's throw from St. Peter's Basilica. You can see all of Rome from there. It was—as we said back then—the proverbial chick magnet, and a day didn't go by that Max invited his pick of traveling tourists, all female of course, up to his 'humble abode.'"

Frazier shrugged. "Well, boy. As they say, when in Rome."

"Yes, and as they said in *Casablanca*, 'it was the beginning of a beautiful friendship.'"

Jonas and Max grinned at each other like there were many more stories to be told, some of which would never come up unless a bartender had been heavy-handed.

"But that doesn't explain Mr. Frazier's reception at the police station," Higgins said.

"Please, call me Max."

"I'm sorry, Max, but why were they treating you that way?"

Max motioned for Jonas to explain.

"I know you're not much into TV, Doc, but while we

Americans have the Kardashians, the Austrians have none other than our host, Prince Maximilian Frazier."

Max did a little bow.

"So you're a reality star?" Neil asked with a grin.

"I prefer the term social entrepreneur," Max said haughtily and then laughed. "It's all nonsense really. My family hates it, but I will say that it has its perks. One of those perks was finding out through my vast network of socialite friends that a certain billionaire and his two friends were being held by Viennese police. When I inquired into the nature of said billionaire's apprehension, I was told that it was a matter of state security. Well, one call led to another, and before you knew it, I was leaving the beautiful blonde who is in my bed and was coming to play shining knight for my good friend, Jonas."

Dr. Higgins shook his head in wonder. Not an hour before, he'd been prepping himself for intense interrogation. He thought that the rescuers would be either Cal and Daniel, maybe President Zimmer himself, but not in his wildest dreams would he have imagined that a celebrity of royal Austrian descent would be their savior.

"On behalf of myself and my companions, I would like to thank you for your generosity," Dr. Higgins said.

"Are you always so formal?" Max asked.

Dr. Higgins sniffed, almost imitating Max's faux royal demeanor. "Someone has to keep these..." and he pointed to Jonas and Neil "...savages civilized. Don't you agree?"

Max laughed out loud and honked his horn three times. "Oh, I'm going to like you very much, Doctor. Very much."

CHAPTER TWENTY-ONE

The bad news kept rolling in. Rourke digested this as well as he could. His men and the handful of women he employed weren't used to him getting frazzled, but frazzled was how he felt.

He'd taken on this job partly as a favor and partly as just another gig. Rourke didn't lean one way or the other politically. He'd made it a point to stay neutral from day one.

Back in the FBI, especially after 9/11, it was popular to let people know whether you were conservative or liberal. Even though everyone wore the American flag, Rourke had never played those games. Straight-laced and by the book, Rourke considered himself incorruptible. He would never take on a job that had the slightest smell of being illegal. While sometimes motives behind his employers were distasteful, Rourke looked at it with a lens of a dispassionate investigator. If two politicians wanted to trash each other, that was their business.

It was just Rourke's job to find the information. Whether the trail led to a coke-sniffing cousin or a story about a would-be Senator beating up a college freshman his first year at

Harvard, Rourke didn't care. His job was to uncover the truth.

Take this job for example; he'd been told to find the link and he'd found it. He had nothing against the men at The Jefferson Group, and to be honest, he actually admired them on some level. Each was a hero in his own right, but they were all connected to the president, and the president was using the organization for his own secret agenda. Rourke hadn't dived into the files yet, just enough to know Cal Stokes and his cohorts functioned under the President of the United States.

It was that revelation that allowed Rourke to take follow-on instructions from Congressman McKnight. He had surreptitiously accessed The Jefferson Group's network. He'd arranged the arrest of the three men in Vienna, and he then attempted apprehension of Cal Stokes and his friends. No one was supposed to be harmed, just brought in so that the authorities could do their work.

Rourke had no endgame except to see the job done. Now a series of complete fuck-ups were threatening to derail Rourke's plans.

Trent and his companion in Amsterdam still hadn't been found. The last they'd been seen, they were jumping into a damned canal. Rourke's man on the ground hadn't thought it wise to go in after them. Right or wrong, he'd lost them.

Then there was the snafu happening in Vienna. He's been assured that there was no way Layton, Patel, and Higgins would be released. Against all odds, like a miracle from freaking heaven, some Austrian celebrity asshole just strolled in and was allowed to take the three with him. Of course, he would have the identification of some prince named Maximilian Frazier the Fifth. *Who calls their kid the fifth anymore?*

Rourke took a deep breath as he replayed the conversation with his man in Vienna. They tried to follow, after the

three captives had been released, but once again the men of
The Jefferson Group had shaken the tail. His men were trying
to locate this Maximilian Frazier now. While the man was
some kind of tabloid celebrity, Rourke's experienced investi-
gators were having a hard time pinpointing exactly where the
man lived.

Now here he was holding all the information that would
torpedo not only The Jefferson Group but also possibly the
President of the United States. Rourke couldn't turn over the
logs until he'd located the culprits. It had been McKnight's
final request. The documents weren't enough, and Rourke
had correctly guessed why McKnight wanted both. It was one
thing to stand up in front of the cameras and wave a few
pieces of paper. It was quite another to have those papers in
hand and in the other hand hold the mug shots of seven
mercenaries. McKnight wanted the one-two punch; who was
Rourke to deny him that? He had to finish the job.

Then it crept out again, that nagging doubt: not whether
he was doing the right thing, but whether he was endangering
a life that shouldn't have been mixed up in his operation.
Anna's life was one he'd sworn to protect two years previ-
ously, and hers was a life that deserved to go on. How had she
gotten mixed up in all this?

Rourke was just thinking that maybe he should put in a
call with some old friends at the Bureau and see if he could
reel his way into a pension, maybe get a gold banner, when his
phone rang again. "This better be good," Rourke said.

"We have them at the Gare du Nord," said Maurice.

"Where? In English, please," Rourke knew that Maurice
liked to flaunt the fact that his American employer couldn't
speak French, so he used it whenever possible.

"It's one of the main train stations here in Paris. You
Americans call it the Paris North."

"How did you find them?"

"I have friends," was Maurice's only reply.

Rourke didn't ask who his friends were. It didn't matter at the moment, although he was impressed that Maurice had tracked them down. Not impressed enough to forget about Maurice's screw-up in the hotel, but maybe one step in the right direction.

"Who's with them?" Rourke asked, hoping it would only be Stokes, his female companion, and the Briggs fellow.

"It was the same four people with the dog, of course: two men and two women."

"Is that right?" Rourke asked, just to confirm.

"Oui," said Maurice.

"Do you have eyes on them now?"

"No, I'm on my way. I'll be there in, say, ten minutes."

"Okay, I'll meet you there. I'll call when I'm close."

Rourke ended the call and thought about shooting McKnight an update, but then thought better of it. McKnight didn't know about all the screw-ups. He just believed that Rourke had the persons of interest and, at the moment, that was all that mattered. Now, to tie up some loose ends and somehow see if he could extract Anna from the proverbial sinking ship ....

CHAPTER TWENTY-TWO

G aucho hadn't really slept. It was hard to with one eye on the door. Mentally, he was sifting through contingencies. What had begun as a relaxing vacation overseas had turned into a complete shit show.

He and Top had talked about contacting someone, but when they tried to call back to Charlottesville, there had been no answer. That could only mean one thing. Although both men were loath to admit it. But, while tossing and turning on Lydia's couch, that's all that Gaucho could think about as he tried to come up with a solution.

Another option was to call the president. However, there was no guarantee that the operator would let them through. Cal was really the only one that had direct access. He was the key. It was safer that way in order to protect the president. It also protected them, but if the entire Jefferson Group was down, the president would have to know about it.

Really it was a moot point. What could Gaucho and Top do? Call the president and say, "Hey, send us a rescue team." No, this is what he'd been trained for. Well, not this exact scenario, but Gaucho was confident in his abilities and those of his best friend lying on the floor just below him.

To Gaucho's surprise, Lydia was the first one up, padding into the kitchen to start some coffee.

"Good morning one and all," Top said from the floor, stretching his huge frame and letting out a stifled yawn. "Please tell me you buy the extra strong stuff at the store, Lydia."

"I always do," Lydia said, smiling at the two men as she busied herself in the kitchen.

Gaucho sat up and cracked his neck from side to side. It wasn't the first night he'd spent restless. However, he'd found that as he'd gotten older, he needed the sleep more and more. He'd always heard that old people needed less sleep, but as his aging body was telling him, he needed more. "Did you come up with any brilliant ideas last night?" he asked.

"Who me?" Top asked, flipping over and doing a quick round of ten push-ups. "I thought you were supposed to be the idea guy."

"I think we have two options," Gaucho said. "We either need to get home, or we need to get to Paris."

"Not Vienna?" Top asked, as he flipped around again and began doing crunches on the ground.

"I hate to leave those guys out there like that," Gaucho said. "But, I think our first responsibility needs to be to link back up with Cal and Daniel. Either that, or we go straight to "you know who" back home."

Being a small outfit meant they could stay nimble and do things below the radar. But it also meant when things went south, their options were limited. They'd all known that going in, but they'd all been volunteers. Besides, the chance of something like this happening was.... Well, they would have said slim to none just two days prior.

"Then Paris it is," Top said hopping to his feet and transitioning into slow and controlled squats.

"Okay, the question is how to get there. We still have fake passports."

"Going anywhere near a major transportation hub would be too obvious," Lydia spoke up from the kitchen, where she was pouring hot water into the French press. "My friend said we could borrow his car. I emailed him this morning, and he said he won't be using it. So, we can take it."

Top stopped his exercises and looked at her. "When you say we, you mean *we?*" He drew a circle around the room to mean all of them as we. Now he pointed back and forth between he and Gaucho.

Lydia mimicked the circle motion with her hand.

"No way, honey. I appreciate the gesture but there are some bad men after us, and I don't want you getting involved."

Lydia set the lid on the French press and left it on the counter. "Are you saying that because I'm a girl, or because you're worried about me?" Lydia asked, one eyebrow raised.

"The latter," Top answered.

"Well, I know these roads really well, and I've driven his car before," she explained. "When you see the auto, you'll know I'm right. It will look more natural for me to be driving, and then you could try to get some sleep. Keep your head down or whatever it is you do when something like this happens."

Top looked to Gaucho, who did the only thing he could figure to do, which was shrug. "We do need to get out of town," Gaucho said. He asked Lydia, "Is there any way that you could bring the car here so ..."

"So you could slip in without being seen?" she finished for him. "Yeah, my friend should be here in fifteen minutes. I told him that I'd probably be in the shower, so just to leave the car in the parking lot with the keys under the mat."

"Well, haven't you just thought of everything?" Gaucho said.

"I told you buddy. She's a smart girl."

"Okay, it's a deal. You drive us far enough, and on the way we'll figure out a way to get all the way to Paris."

True to her word, the car was there in fifteen minutes. By then, everyone had had their fill of coffee and had prepared for the journey. Not that there was much to take. Their clothes and the rest of their belongings were still at the hotel for all they knew. Lydia was kind enough to pack a small bag with snacks and drinks for the road.

When the text came through that her friend had dropped off the car, Lydia grabbed her bag and left the flat to retrieve the car. A light tap of the horn a couple of minutes later indicated that she was out front. So Gaucho and Top exited to find Lydia idling one of those miniature European cars.

Top chuckled, "I get the front seat, brother."

There was barely a back seat, and when Gaucho squeezed in, he wondered if he'd ever again have feeling in his legs. Willy had to push his seat all the way back which meant that Gaucho was kind of scrunched up in the back. He didn't complain. It would be rude and besides, Lydia was helping them. Who was he to complain?

"Would you like to do the honors, my lady?" Top said.

Lydia put the car in drive and Gaucho was happy to hear the gear shift was smooth and the engine purred along happily. They pulled out of the small courtyard and were on their way towards Paris. No detection.

What the three companions couldn't have known was that four blocks away, in a vacant office building, stood a man behind a telescopic lens. He was wearing a blue track suit today and as he clicked away, he reached for his phone. When the car was out of sight, he dialed the number and said three words, "I've got them." Then he ended the call, took the camera from the tripod, removed the long lens, and deposited everything into a black duffle bag.

Two minutes later, he was pulling out of his own court-yard. Taking his time, he was confident that the beacon one of his men had put on the undercarriage of the car would go undetected and allow him a leisurely drive through the Dutch countryside.

CHAPTER TWENTY-THREE

The Bentley weaved its way through the maze of the
Vienna streets. They were going in the opposite direction of most of the traffic, and soon found themselves in residential neighborhoods that in some ways reminded Jonas of
the Pacific Palisades – hilly and exclusive. There was no
beach, but there was plenty of money with large homes
settled closely together.

He figured that Max was probably taking them to one of
his many homes. He didn't live in them all, but he had tenants
and Max would occasionally slip in to say hello. He remembered one particular visit when Max had taken Jonas to a
vacant property that was about to be rented and proceeded to
call every socialite he knew. Max booked a band that was
currently playing on Austrian radio, and a full complement of
drinks and hors d'oeuvres from a local restaurant. That was
Maximilian Frazier. He could snap his fingers and things
would happen. Even before Jonas knew Max had money, there
was just an air about him that was hard not to be drawn to. It
was no wonder he'd become such a sensation in his home
country.

They'd stayed in contact over the years, visiting each other when possible. There'd even been talk of a business deal or two; however, nothing had solidified. Max didn't need the money, and in many ways Jonas didn't want to endanger their friendship by involving business. Not that it couldn't happen, and not that he wasn't in business with friends, but Max had a way of being all-in one second and then flitting to another idea the next. It had been at least a year since Jonas had seen him, but from the car and the attire, it looked like Max hadn't changed.

"That vineyard there has been in my family for three generations," Max said, pointing as they passed a walled compound on the right. Jonas took his word for it. Whereas in America a vineyard would have splashed its name and logo on every corner, in Europe, and in Vienna particularly, it was sometimes hard to distinguish what company lay inside a building or a given property. Everything felt understated. It was as if they didn't want the extra business.

Further up the steep hill they went, and then Max turned into a narrow drive that looked like it could barely handle a vehicle. To prove Jonas's point, Max tapped a button and the side mirrors folded in. This drive was even steeper than the last, and up the incline the car climbed. There were fields of grapevines on their left and a high white wall on their right. Max pulled off to the left not far up the hill.

"Here we are," he announced. He pulled a set of keys from his pocket and went to a large wooden door that might have been the entrance to either a house or a business. When they went inside, Max locked the door behind them. Jonas noted the stone walls as if they'd been carved from the hill itself. It felt cold inside, like they were in a cave.

When they went into the main room, there was a long bar with tables set off to the side. Each tabletop had vases full of wilting flowers. "Well, do you like it?" Max asked, flipping on light switches and gesturing the space beyond and to the large glass window, floor-to-ceiling located at the far end of the room, and Jonas walked that way.

"Do you live here?" Neil asked.

"No, of course not; it's an old winery and used to belong to one of my competitors, but I just closed on the property yesterday and hadn't had time to come by. Would anybody like a glass of wine?" he said, grabbing two bottles from behind the bar.

"Don't you think it's a little early for that?" Jonas asked, marveling at the view of all of Vienna in the distance.

"You're right," Max said, "We should go with beer." And as the other three took in the view, Max poured them foaming drafts in Bavarian-style mugs. Then he walked to the end of the room, handing a mug to each man. "To old friends and new," Max said, raising his mug.

"And to our host, for getting us out of the clink," Neil said, raising his mug and clinking his against Max's.

Jonas was in no mood to have a beer this early in the morning, but he went along with his friends, surprised that even Dr. Higgins swallowed his drink hungrily, and that's when Jonas realized that'd been the point through it all. That's what people didn't realize about Max, there was always a point. He'd recognized that his guests needed to relax, so he brought them here, somewhere private, somewhere where they could share a beer and talk in quiet and forget about their earlier misfortunes.

"Come, we should go outside. It's a beautiful morning and it's a much better view from out there." Jonas was halfway through his beer, relishing the brisk breeze sweeping across the hillside when Max finally asked, "Are you going to tell me or do I have to pry it out of you?"

"Tell you what?" Jonas asked, apparently forgetting where they'd been.

"Are you playing coy, or has that beer already gone to your head?" Max said with a grin.

Jonas shook his head. "I'm sorry Max, but I really don't think we should tell you. We appreciate your help, but you don't want to get mixed up in this."

Max put his hands to his chest and staggered back like he'd been wounded. "After everything we've been through?"

"Come on Max. It's not like that. And besides, we really don't know the whole picture either."

Max righted himself and took a long, long pull from his beer. When he'd drained the mug, he looked to his friend again. "A little birdy told me that it was Americans who pressured the Austrian police to arrest you. Would you like to know the name of my little birdy who tipped me off?" Jonas nodded. "We Austrians don't take kindly to foreigners. Americans are not supposed to be telling us Austrians our business. So naturally when I contacted my good friend, the police commissioner, he was more than happy to tell me that some well-connected Americans were trying to run his show."

Jonas wasn't surprised that Max knew the police commissioner, but he was surprised that the commissioner had seen fit to divulge that type of information. "And this commissioner, you know him because?"

"Oh, we run in the same circles. He likes wine; I like wine. He likes pretty women; I know a lot of pretty women. So naturally, we've become friends."

"Did he say who they worked for?"

"I asked but he didn't know. He said a call came in from our government. He was ordered to cooperate. That was three days ago."

Three days, Jonas thought. So, that meant they probably had been watched the entire time they'd been in Vienna.

Jonas shivered at the thought. Cal was always telling him to be careful, to be deliberate, and to remember where he'd been and who he'd seen. Jonas had cast it off as the normal paranoia of a warrior, accustomed to operating behind enemy lines. Now he understood that any one of the hundreds of students he'd talked to over the past two days could have been watching him. Not because they wanted to learn from a billionaire, but because they were tracking him.

"Was it your commissioner friend who allowed us to leave?" Dr. Higgins asked.

"Not exactly," Max answered. "As I told you before, a friend of a friend did me that favor, but the commissioner was only too happy to oblige. I'm sure he's getting an earful now, but he'll sit there and take it knowing that he made me and my friends happy."

"In that case I think we should probably go," Jonas said. "You've done enough Max, and I really appreciate it, but we really need to get all of our friends together."

"Is there any way I can help?" Max asked.

"You wouldn't by any chance have a way of getting us to Paris, would you? Undetected, I might add."

"It just so happens that I might have just the thing. Come, my home is not far from here."

Max's current home turned out to be a mansion on the far side of the ravine from the vineyard they'd visited. As they pulled in, Frazier reported that the American Ambassador to Austria was the neighbor on his left, and the Japanese Ambassador lived to his right.

"Your ambassador is quite the snob," Max said. "The Japanese ambassador, however, let's just say I understand why he keeps so young." Max winked at his friend and then pulled up to the front step of the house.

They got out and were greeted by a man in full livery. He said something to Max in his native tongue. Max replied and the manservant got in the Bentley and drove somewhere out of sight. "Would you like a hot shower or a change of clothes before you leave?" Max asked as they entered the house. The inside of Max's home was as exactly as Jonas would have expected. It had cavernous ceilings and priceless paintings adorning the walls.

"I could use a shower," Neil said.

"I wouldn't mind one either," Dr. Higgins added.

Jonas would have leaned the opposite way, but he recognized that his friends were tired. The luxurious home and its aristocratic touches called at least Dr. Higgins to explore. "I'll take a shower too," Jonas said, realizing that they probably had some time.

Max showed them each to a separate rooms, and although Jonas told himself that he would only be in the shower for a moment, he found himself marinating in the blissfully hot water for what turned out to be twenty minutes. He emerged from the bathroom. His clothes were gone, but there was a white terrycloth robe and a glass of champagne sitting on a trunk at the end of the bed. Jonas slipped into the robe and grabbed the glass of wine. He sipped it as he wound his way down the long hall and found his friends in the main living area. It was a massive room with an impressive collection of comfortable sofas and elegant sitting chairs. Dr. Higgins was chatting away with Max when Jonas entered, and Neil was clacking away at his laptop.

"I'm sorry I took so long," Jonas said, "That shower felt amazing." That's when he noticed that his two American companions were also wearing white robes. "Where did our clothes go?" Jonas asked.

"My housekeeper is washing them. I thought you might like to hit the road in clean attire. It won't take long."

Jonas was about to protest. The shower had revived him and now he felt like they needed to hit the road. They needed to find Cal and Daniel, and then somehow link up with Trent and Gaucho.

What had seemed like a brilliant idea, spreading out over Europe, had turned out to be a real pain. Their team was in pieces, but Jonas had to remind himself that the others could take care of themselves. In fact, he, Dr. Higgins, and Neil were probably the least prepared for what had happened. That made him even more grateful for Max's intercession.

"You said something about a way out of here?" Jonas said.

Max snapped his fingers and hopped up from the sofa, "Right, come." He motioned to the window and Jonas followed him. When they'd reached the massive glass panes that overlooked the vineyards beyond, Max pointed down the hill and Jonas's eyes followed the gesture. There, parked on a plateau of perfectly manicured grass, was a helicopter.

"My pilot is on the way," Max said. "He'll take you wherever you need to go. I've also alerted my team at the Vienna airport. It's a private runway, of course; they're at your disposal, and have been given instructions to grease the way through customs in whichever country you decide to fly to."

"Max, I don't know how to..."

The socialite put up his hand. "It's what friends do, Jonas. Just don't forget about me the next time you want to start a business in Europe." The two men grinned at each other.

True to his word, thirty minutes later the pilot arrived. Wearing freshly laundered clothes, the three Americans piled into the surprisingly spacious helicopter. "You'll call me when everything's settled," Max said over the whine of the starting helicopter.

"Yeah, and thank you again!" Jonas shouted back.

Max nodded and slammed the door shut, stepping away from the rotors that were now turning overhead. They picked up speed, and less than a minute later they lifted off, the three friends in the back waving to their host.

When the helicopter had flown out of sight, Max extracted a cell phone from his pocket and placed a call. There was a curt greeting on the other end and then Max said, "Tell the Americans that they've left and that they're headed to Paris."

CHAPTER TWENTY-FOUR

"I think we need to plan for the worst, Mr. President."

President Brandon Zimmer looked up from his desk, annoyance written all over his face. "A second ago you were calling me Brandon, Marge, and now back to this Mr. President business. Why do I have a feeling this is a precursor to you telling me something I don't want to hear? Just give it to me straight."

"I always do, you know that. Fine, I'll say it. We haven't heard from Cal in hours. I know that may not seem like a long time, but in his line of work, combined with the fact that we didn't hear from anyone else in The Jefferson Group, we should assume the worst."

"Marge, why don't we focus on the campaign instead?" It's what he'd been doing all day. At least one thing was going well. "I've got faith in Cal, and I'm sure he knows what he's doing. If there's anything I've learned, it's to not second guess them. You of all people should know that."

Marge Haines nodded, but it felt like she was shrewdly analyzing the commander in chief. "That still doesn't mean we shouldn't prepare," she said finally. "In case things go from bad to worse."

The president snapped the pencil in his hand and stated: "Those men have done more for me than anyone has, damn it, and I will not sell them out!"

"I didn't say anything about selling them out, Mr. President."

"I said don't call me that, goddamn it! You're Marge, I'm Brandon. We're having a conversation about our friends Cal, Daniel, Top, Gaucho, Dr. Higgins, Neal, Jonas, and hell, even Diane's with them!" Zimmer threw the broken pencil into the trash can and willed himself to take a deep breath to purge the anger. "I'm sorry, I shouldn't have snapped at you, it's just that..."

"I know," Marge said, "They're my friends too, remember?"

The president nodded absently. While there were so many facets of his job that he loved, places where he knew he could make a difference, he could never shake the feeling that no matter how much he tried, there was still a huge hole being dug somewhere else and once he left office, all his gains would be thrown in that hole and covered up for eternity.

The Jefferson Group was just one of those advancements. A small group dedicated to doing the right thing. He'd learned so much from those men. There'd been close calls before. They'd suffered heavy losses, primarily his chief of staff, Travis Hayden, on one of their missions. Zimmer knew something felt different.

While it was the commander in chief's job to stay optimistic, he couldn't help but let his mind slide down the off-ramp of pessimism. "Let's just get one thing straight," Zimmer began and then he smiled. "I want you to tell me the truth, you know that? Right now, your bedside manner could use a little work. That's me being honest, one friend to another."

Marge nodded. "It's the lawyer in me coming out. I was trained to look at things through a dispassionate lens, and sometimes that, well, it makes me come off rather harsh, and I apologize."

"There's no need," said the president. "Now, tell me what you were thinking."

Marge quickly outlined her contingency plan. It basically meant denying the fact that The Jefferson Group ever existed, and while Zimmer would hold onto that as a last resort, he never wanted to use that option. Cal would understand if he had to, of course, but Brandon could taste the bile rising in the back of his throat just thinking about it.

It was a classic politician move and being a classic politician was anything but what he wanted. He let Marge speak and when she'd finished, he swallowed and said, "Thank you for your candor, Marge. I don't ever want you to feel like you can't tell me what you're thinking. It's your job and if I ever make you feel otherwise, push back on my stubborn pigheadedness and get to the heart of it."

"Can I get that in writing?" Marge asked finally, cracking a smile.

"Would you like that handwritten, or should I have my secretary type it up in the morning?" They both laughed at the lame attempt to make a joke designed to share more than their nervous energy. They had expressions of actual mirth. "If we ever get a second to get out of here and get some shuteye, I'll think about it Marge. I promise you I will."

"Why don't we back up by discussing what we have going on the campaign stops tomorrow?" Marge slipped an itinerary from the bottom of the pile on her desk and held it up.

The president could see that his schedule was full and he somehow held back an exhausted moan then he brightened and said, "You know I almost feel bad for Tony McKnight. He's really kept his word, you know, and here we are whipping him in every poll we can find. It's almost too easy, really..." Then the president paused, his mind driving down a dangerous path.

It was almost October, and October was notorious for election surprises. He thought about Cal's two words, "Liberty down." Liberty down...Liberty down. Could it be someone's first shot at his campaign? *No, that was too much of a leap.*

He shook the thought away. It was just coincidence. It had to be, because if it wasn't, well, he couldn't think about that now. "Let's talk about the debate. I know the Congressman's been obliging, but I don't think a CNN moderator will be so kind."

As Marge discussed the next day's activities and what she believed should be the president's key points during the upcoming debate, Zimmer could only think about where his friend Cal was and how this might all tie back to him.

CHAPTER TWENTY-FIVE

"I'm sorry you got dragged into this," Daniel whispered to Anna, who was resting her head on his shoulder. She was wrapped in his coat. It was the best they could do to fend off the breeze blowing in from the open side of the train station.

Anna didn't look up, but said "You really know how to show an old friend a good time, don't you?" she joked.

"Is that what we are? Old friends? Sounds funny to say," Daniel quipped. "Me, I might be old, but you?"

Anna lifted her head and looked up at him, with those piercing eyes that saw right through him. Like that first morning so many years before when he'd felt that the world held no place for him, but one teenage girl held out hope, much like she was doing now.

"I'm not that young, you know," she said, "besides, you don't look like you've aged a day. The years have been good to you, Daniel. I mean that."

Daniel pretended to take the compliment in stride, but he had the acute feeling every time she talked to him that his Zen-like world was being rattled. Control was his thing. Of course, he was human, and only an idiot would say they never got scared. However, Daniel had learned to harness that fear, bending and twisting it to his will.

He looked down at Anna but the spell was broken now as an announcement sounded overhead. Anna perked up, listening. "Our train is finally here," she said. It had been delayed, and the ticking minutes had done nothing to help the others' already frazzled nerves.

Cal seemed to be taking the worst of it. It was not that he'd worried about the danger, but the heaping plate of responsibility was squarely at his table setting.

Daniel had discussed this with him, and they'd come to the agreement that the president would have to wait. First, they had to get the team back together. They had to make sure everyone was okay, and then they would contact the White House. Only then would they go after whoever had brought The Jefferson Group to its knees.

"Do you want another coffee before we go?" Daniel asked Anna.

"I'll take one if you're going," Diane said next to him.

"Me too," said Anna.

"Two coffees. Cal, you want anything?" Daniel asked.

Cal shook his head. "I'll get something on the train."

His friend's face was strained, so Daniel smiled at him. "I'll be right back. Diane, make sure Cal takes a potty break before we get on the train. You never know with those train restrooms."

Cal looked up at him in surprise. Daniel wasn't the joke teller, but the Marine realized what his friend had done. It was one thing to be on edge, yet it was quite another to lose control. Daniel had let Cal know he was straddling that fine line; Cal nodded his gratitude to Daniel.

The line at the nearest café was long. Daniel veered to the left and went further into the train station, always scanning the area as he went, although no one could pick up on his subtle examination of his environment.

While his exterior looked placid, bordering on boredom, the Beast inside Daniel growled as it sniffed the air, hoping for a target. Daniel wouldn't consider himself friends with his inner demon; it wasn't that sort of relationship.

Back in the bad days, the Beast had been in control, and Daniel never had a say in its actions. It had been like unleashing a rabid panther in downtown Tokyo when the Beast targeted blood. But when Daniel regained control, once again assuming the role of Master, the two came to an understanding, of sorts. The Beast would lend itself to Daniel, allowing him to use its skill, and in exchange Daniel would not kill it.

Daniel knew he could kill it. The Beast would probably be diagnosed by some psychologist as a figment of his imagination or a projection of his innermost fears. However, Daniel didn't view that primitive being in that way. He imagined the great Beast walking next to him, licking the air, its penetrating gaze silently interrogating anyone who passed by. Daniel walked with his invisible friend taking everything in, and the Beast provided protection.

The tourists rushed to catch their trains, and an old woman struggled to carry a small dog in her left arm while pulling a wheeled cart with her right. He had just reached the line of two people anxiously waiting for their coffee when his body felt an electric shock of warning. Daniel looked around casually but didn't see anything. That didn't mean it wasn't there.

He looked deeper, searching the eyes of passersby, trusting his instincts. He provided the Beast a little more chain to walk on, and then he saw the danger. He spotted three girls probably in their mid-to-late twenties, approximately Anna's age. They had the slightly darker complexions of Middle-Easterners. However, they just as easily might have been from Turkey, Syria, or even born natives of France. There was a huge population of immigrants all over Paris's streets.

The girls were dressed like thousands of other young women in the city. In casual clothes, they looked like they might be going on vacation or waiting to hop on a train to visit a friend. All three wore tight jeans, athletic shoes and each also wore a black backpack and pulled a pink rolling bag. They were matching, strike one. But then again, it could be nothing. They should have been chatting contentedly, but Daniel felt (without seeing) the strain among them - much like Cal was behaving a moment ago.

Although passersby might see it as remnants of an argument within the girls group, or maybe one of them had forgotten something at her home, Daniel knew better. He ignored the woman at the café counter and walked away from the stand, taking a roundabout route toward the three young women.

As he got closer, the menace punctured his senses like the smell coming from a rotting corpse. The girls were trying too hard to appear calm, probably something they had routinely practiced; Daniel saw right through it. One girl, after throwing a furtive glance up at the train station's information board as if searching for something, turned and said something to her friends before she walked off. There were no hugs exchanged and no long goodbyes. There was just a curt nod and off she walked. Daniel noticed her face was fraught with anticipation. Since the two remaining young women didn't look like they were moving anytime soon, Daniel followed the first girl to depart the group.

She made her way down the escalators to the lower level. Daniel decided to hustle by her, as if late for his train. But when he walked by, he glanced down and took a full measure of the woman. He observed that despite the cold morning, a thin sheen of perspiration covered the back of her neck and her brow. She had white headphone cords looped over the back of her neck, dangling down, ready for use. That morning she looked like any other traveler, bound for destinations unknown.

Daniel measured her strides and fell back as if he'd dropped something. He pulled a pen out of his pocket and rushed to catch up with her. He tapped her on the shoulder, and she whipped around so fast it was like she'd heard a gunshot. He observed she had the wide eyes of a scared animal.

"Excuse me, did you drop this?" Daniel said, showing her the pen. It took her a few moments to compose herself, but in that time, Daniel saw everything he needed to see. "What? No," she said in heavily accented English. "Excuse me, but I have a train to catch." She turned on her heel and hurried off.

Daniel weighed his options. If he had been in America, under quite different circumstances, he would not have hesitated to attack the girl. However, this was France, and he was on the run. Luckily, there was a pair of policemen nearby. "Excuse me, do you speak English?"

"Yes," the one on the right said politely, "How can I help you sir?"

"I don't know how to say this. I don't know how the rules work here, but that girl over there walking with the pink bag. I think she has something, something dangerous."

The two policemen were instantly on alert. One of them didn't hesitate to put in a call on the radio. "What did you see, Monsieur?"

"I don't know," Daniel stuttered, going with the stupid American routine, "there was a wire in her hand. It was attached to her phone. I can't be sure, but I wouldn't want anything to happen."

That was all the police needed. They left Daniel where he was and sprinted to find the girl. When Daniel was sure the focus was no longer on him, he pivoted and sprinted back from where he'd come, hoping to God he wouldn't be too late to thwart a probable terrorist plot.

CHAPTER TWENTY-SIX

The first would-be bomber came from an unlikely background. When she'd first arrived at the training camp in Pakistan, she'd been quiet to the point of seeming mute. The trainers had harassed her day and night, thinking that maybe they'd keep her as a slave to clean the toilets or use her as a real-life dummy in a training simulation. It had taken the intercession of the camp commander himself to stop the harassment. When he'd reviewed her file, he'd been pleased to find an unassuming young woman from a good family. She had done well in school, but for the most part kept to herself.

While many under his command screamed their allegiance to Allah day and night, the commander knew the truth. Most of the recruits he received were young, inexperienced and used bravado to mask their fear. Some would piss their pants. Many would cry at night, at moments proclaiming "death to the white infidels."

Not this girl. There had been no incidents, and in fact, as he dug deeper, the commander saw that the quiet one had met, and often excelled, at many of the requirements even his male recruits found difficult.

One of the first things he banished when he had taken command was the outright harassment of female recruits. His people were prejudiced, he knew. They put women in what was considered their place. It was part of their culture, but the camp commander was of the modern breed. He'd grown up in the West, had classmates who were women, and respected them for their honesty and bravery in the face of overwhelming odds, and so he'd selected the quiet girl as one of his special projects. In her way, she'd accepted it, and much to her own surprise, had been dubbed one of the leaders of the battle in her home city of Paris, France.

She'd been startled by the blonde stranger, who'd asked about the dropped pen, and other than that misunderstanding and the sweat glazing her body, the quiet one moved along with supreme confidence. She had blended in perfectly with the crowd. She looked like them, dressed like them, and from the outside at least, she was one of them.

When she'd been sent to Pakistan, she hadn't protested. Her father wouldn't have wanted it that way. Her mother hadn't been surprised. She was their only child, and while the quiet one knew that it hadn't been her parents' idea, the recruitment call had come late one night. She didn't let on that she knew that if she didn't go to Pakistan, trouble would befall her entire family.

So, she'd gone, taken her beatings and the abuse. She suffered the lascivious stares of the male trainees and their leaders. Even the other women had followed up with their own jabs.

Then, with the snap of a finger, everything had changed. The camp commander had taken a liking to her. Once that had happened, "the quiet one," as they now called her, shifted her focus from surviving to thriving. She'd surprised herself with her talents. While many of the women dropped to the ground when they lost their breath or when they scraped a leg jumping over a stone wall, the quiet one kept it all bottled up.

Over the days and then weeks, she'd surpassed her peers and soon they looked to her with grudging respect. On that last night, when they'd been given the final blessing, and the camp commander had taken her into his bed, she'd finally felt full of the things she'd been looking for. That missing piece of her life that she'd never found in Paris, she'd found beneath the stars in Pakistan.

She'd never known the camp commander's real name. They never used names in training. They said it was because American spies were everywhere, but the quiet one believed it was simply easier that way. You didn't want to become too attached, but as she walked along, she thought about the camp commander's kindness and his rule over the undisciplined recruits that had flown in from all over the world. She wondered if they'd have had a chance in another life. Maybe if they'd met on the streets of Islamabad or in a café in Kabul.... The quiet one smiled at that. It was just a dream. It would only be that, never more.

The quiet one wandered into the mass of people in front of her, all waiting for the outgoing trains. Her timing had been perfect, but her timing was always perfect. She'd given explicit instructions to her two companions. Hopefully, they would follow them to completion. She'd almost stayed back to watch them, to make sure they carried out their missions, but the quiet one knew it didn't matter. This day more than one blow would be struck by her people and for her home.

She was about to start her prayer, to ask for that final strength to do what needed to be done, when there was a call from behind her, followed by another. She ignored it at first, but then she noticed that people were looking at her. So she turned calmly, although her heart was thrumming.

There were two police officers running toward her, guns drawn. There'd always been a chance that she'd be discovered, but not like this. She'd done everything correctly; she recalled and ticked off the morning commute, the conversation with her companions, her walk through the train station and she saw no error. Instead of panicking, she just stood there and waited until the two policemen were standing in front of her.

"Madame, may we see your bag please?"

"What have I done?" the quiet one asked innocently.

"The bag, Madame," the policeman said, holding out a hand. The one that didn't have a gun. They weren't pointing weapons at her, not yet. Their muzzles were still pointed at the ground, and that was a good sign.

She looked around at her fellow travelers, purposefully stamping minor panic on her face. People were backing away now. "The bag, Madame," the policeman said louder now. The quiet one saw more police running in her direction. Her time was up. She nodded once to the police officers and raised her hands in the air. Unfortunately, she wouldn't have time to arm the explosives in her carry-on, but she still had her backpack.

As her arms raised slowly, she almost salivated at the look of horror in the officer's face and at the quick intakes of breath from the people around her who noticed the thin wire running from the phone in her hand to her now falling sleeve.

"And now we die," she whispered as she pressed the button.

CHAPTER TWENTY-SEVEN

Ian Rourke and the Frenchman, Maurice, had just walked in the side entrance at the Gare du Nord, when a trio of armored soldiers ran by them.

"What do you think that is?" Rourke asked.

"Probably some homeless men walking on the tracks. It happens all the time, and they treat it like it's a terrorist plot from Osama bin Laden himself," Maurice answered, flicking his cigarette to the ground. Just as Maurice went to fish another one from his pocket, the ground rumbled and shuddered, followed by a boom that sounded like it came from some deep underground cavern.

"What was that?" Rourke asked.

"Probably construction," Maurice said, but he ignored his cigarettes now. They kept walking. Nothing seemed amiss. Many of the travelers paused while passing through on their morning commute and then stopped at the sound, but when no alarms came from the overhead speakers, they kept going.

"Where did you say they were?" Rourke asked.

"My friends said they were over by the café along here."

"You didn't tell your friends why we needed help with the video, did you?"

"Of course not," Maurice scoffed, "I said it was a special favor, that a pair of pretty girls took me for some money. They laughed and gave me what I needed."

While Rourke didn't approve of Maurice's tactics, he had to admit that the man was efficient. Not only had he pinpointed Anna's location in the city, he even got confirmation over his phone as to exactly where in the station she and Stokes were. Rourke was about to tell Maurice to go back to the van and join the others. The plan had been for the Frenchman to point the way and stand in reserve. Rourke didn't want to spook Anna or the others. He just wanted to get eyes on to confirm to himself that his quarry had been found. But the next moments changed all that.

The first thing that happened was a recording of a woman's voice on the overhead speakers. It was in French, and while Rourke didn't understand it, the recording's effects were instantaneous. Maurice turned, as did many of the travelers around him.

"We need to go," Maurice said.

"What is it?"

"Probably nothing, but we must go."

"I'm not leaving until...."

"Fine, suit yourself," Maurice said, "I do not want to die today." Without another word, he ran back the way they'd come in. Now there were more people running. Rourke could see by the looks on their faces that it was going to turn into a stampede. He stepped aside and skirted up the far hall and the voice overhead returned, this time in English. "Please proceed to the exits. This is a mandatory evacuation. Please proceed calmly to the exits."

Evacuation? Rourke thought. He picked up his pace, thinking that maybe the police had found Stokes and his companions. Then he thought about the loud boom just after they'd entered. It had to be a terrorist threat. As if the universe wanted to confirm his assessment, a voice from his earpiece came in loud and clear. "Boss, they're reporting multiple attacks around Paris. They've already discovered a few dead and wounded at the train station. We should go."

Rourke ignored his team leader's voice. "Boss, are you there?"

"Yeah, I'm here. Why don't you guys get out of here? I'll meet you back at the lobby and go point."

"Roger that."

But instead of turning around, Rourke headed deeper into the panicked crowds filling the train station, his gun now hanging from his right hand. He had to find Anna.

* * *

"WHAT WAS THAT?" Anna asked. Cal and Diane both looked up at the sound too.

"Where's Daniel?" Cal asked as he jumped to his feet.

"He went to get coffee, remember?"

"I know, but he should be back by now," Cal said. Cal scanned the crowd, which, as yet, had not become panicked.

But then the announcement in French sounded overhead and Anna's face went pale. "They say we need to leave, but we can't. Where's Daniel?" She hopped up on top of the bench and looked the way Daniel had gone. She could barely make out anything in the bustling throng. The announcement could only mean one thing. She knew that sound had been a bomb. They needed to leave, but she wouldn't and couldn't leave Daniel. She feared the worst. Daniel had been part of that explosion. She feared the others had somehow found him and had gone to extreme measures to take out the Marine sniper.

Then she saw him and raised her hands. He was rushing through the crowd, like a lone wolf parting a sea of salmon. When he arrived, Anna wrapped her arms around him. "Oh my God, what happened?" she asked.

"We need to get out of here."

"Did you see it?" Cal asked Daniel.

"I didn't see it, but I knew. I told a couple of cops, and .... Well, I'm sure they're dead. But there are two more attackers, and I lost them in the crowd. They probably scattered when the first bomb went off."

Anna could see that Daniel was torn. He wanted to stay and help. It was what he did. He wanted to protect her, but she wouldn't let him do it. If some people wanted to blow themselves up, let them be. Anna knew there were typically fail-safes, even if the attackers were shot, something would still explode.

"We need to get help," Cal said, "you two should go. Daniel and I are going see if we can help."

"But you're not even armed!" Diane protested.

Cal grinned. "We'll figure it out. We always do."

Daniel was about to add to Cal's assessment when Diane said, "No. I'm coming with you. Honey, you're not listening to me, I'm coming with you."

There were screams now at the bombing level of the train station. The tension between Cal and Diane evaporated at the sounds.

"You need to go," Daniel said to Anna so only she could hear.

"No," she said without thinking, "I'm staying with you, too."

To his credit, Daniel didn't protest and in that moment, Anna felt a flood of emotion wash over her. Their collective minds made up, Cal asked, "Which way do you think they went?"

"My guess would be the exits; they didn't seem like the stay-and-fight type."

Anna was about to ask Daniel how he knew that. They were already moving. Daniel took the lead, cutting a path through the throng of flesh. They felt another explosion, closer this time. While Anna ducked, Daniel barely flinched, still bustling forward through the crowd around him. To match Anna's mood, there was crying all around, screams. Mothers, children, businessmen. Anna's body shook. She knew at any moment they could be dead. She somehow willed her legs to keep moving, one hand clutched tightly with Daniel's, pulling her forward, and they went into the smoke, closer to the bloody madness.

* * *

IAN ROURKE DIDN'T STOP MOVING when the second explosion went off either. He started running, with no idea where Anna might be. No thoughts of surveilling; Stokes and Daniel Briggs had flown from his thoughts. Then he saw her up ahead in the mass of the crowd, being pulled forward, her jet-black hair like a beacon to him. He cut away from the wall, about to come up behind them. It was the most direct route with much of the crowd having dispersed behind them. Rourke caught up quickly. He saw Daniel Briggs in the lead, Stokes pulling the girl, Diane Mayer, along behind him.

Their focus was forward, with the carnage, and while that might have given Rourke pause on a normal day, on this day he took it as a blessing. He could sneak up completely undetected. While he still didn't know what he was going to do or say, he knew he had to close the gap. About twenty feet separated them now.

Rourke weighed his options. As far as he knew, Stokes and Briggs weren't armed. That meant Rourke had the upper hand, but what was he going to do? Shoot them? No. All their indiscretions aside, Rourke wasn't going to do that. As far as he knew, they were decent men who had done some illegal things. They'd still served their country. Besides, gunshots would give Rourke away and that was the last thing he needed.

Ten feet away. Maybe he should call out to her, but he was unsure she'd recognize him. The night before when they'd run from the hotel, he'd come sprinting out the opposite side of the street.

In the end, Rourke didn't make the choice. Someone made it for him. Something hit him from behind, and he was tackled to the floor. He went with it, pitching forward, pushing past. When he got back to his feet, there was yelling from where he'd just been.

Four police officers, their weapons leveled. That was when Rourke realized he had the weapon in his hand. They were screaming in French so he didn't understand them, but their objective was plain. They wanted him to put down the weapon.

Instead of complying with their orders, he looked left to where the moving group of four now turned and were staring at the confrontation. Rourke's eyes met Anna's and her face paled. His heart sank. It was clear that she thought he was the enemy, as did the police. He started to raise his hands in the air to assuage the police; also to show Anna he meant no threat.

Then there was movement to the left of Anna. Most of the crowd was either on their stomachs on the ground or in a crouch, but there was a young woman wearing a backpack, with a pink rolling case in her left hand who was obviously panicked. For some reason, Rourke couldn't take his eyes off her.

One of the French police had taken to yelling at him in

English, and indeed they were telling him to drop the weapon and lay on the ground. The cop was screaming about another bomb, about his accomplices and where they were.

Then all the pieces in Rourke's mind fit together. He raised the weapon and fired.

* * *

SHE HAD SEEN him the night before. She knew she remembered that face. Ian Rourke had been one of her contacts at the Federal Bureau of Investigation. He'd been a taciturn man, but professional. He'd done his job well. In the end, he'd even become a friend. She'd been young. Rourke had been one of the first liaisons the FBI had sent, but she remembered him vividly.

But now, to see him in the middle of Paris train station, gun in hand, she felt only confusion. That confusion quickly turned to horror. Could Rourke have been behind it all? Was he with the bombers? What was he doing here?

The French police were screaming at Rourke to drop the gun. Rourke ignored them. He was staring at Anna; she couldn't make out the look on his face. Pleading, maybe? Then his gaze shifted away from her. Anna followed his look to a young girl near her own age, her eyes wide with fright. She held the handle of a pink rolling suitcase and wore a black pack on her back. Her eyes flittered around the whole group: the police who were focused on Rourke, who in turn was looking at Anna and her companions.

Anna could sense that something was wrong, and then time slowed. Rourke's weapon came up. Anna's hand reached out to stop him. His weapon fired three times and Anna screamed.

CHAPTER TWENTY-EIGHT

L iberty was finding it nearly impossible to keep up with
Master and keep away from all the moving legs and
stomping feet. She'd already been kicked a handful of times,
and she didn't understand why. She was used to crowds, but
there was something inherently different about this one.

She could smell the fear in the air, knowing that scent
from humans since her first days. She had that gift, that intu-
itive sense of what made humans happy, angry, sad and, especially, fearful.

For example, she knew it made Master happy when she
sat next to him, and as a reward, he would reach down and
stroke her head and neck. Sometimes Liberty would fall
asleep; she liked those moments. They were her favorite
times. That and playing fetch with a ball. At times, she would
become so fixated on the ball she'd forget about the rules,
about making Master angry or even sad. Then she would
catch a glimpse of his face, and she would remember. She
didn't do that for everyone. She was still technically a puppy,
after all.

For all she knew, other humans were important, but they

weren't as important as Master. She loved him unconditionally, even when he was angry with her. Liberty had filed each bit of knowledge away. Taking food from the table was bad, but taking food from the Master's hand was good. Peeing on the corner of a building was bad. Peeing on grass outside of a building was good.

Now all the rules were becoming a confusing mishmash with the jostling and kicking, the screams and the fear. Confusion set her eyes wide. She finally saw him up ahead. There he was; there was Master. He didn't call her name, but he didn't have to. Liberty honestly thought that she could find Master anywhere. She was rarely separated from him, but when she was, she felt like it was the worst thing in the world. It caused her physical pain and it made her want to howl.

Time held no meaning when it was spent away from Master. A minute, an hour, or a day. Those times, she would forget the rules too. Sometimes she would whine, bark, and then howl, like her ancient ancestors in the wild.

But Master was here now, even if he was too far away to touch. Liberty remembered the rules. *Do not bark. Do not whine. Do not howl.* She felt those things welling up inside of her. It was a kind of panic, tempting her to itch, to scratch that need and to bark loudly for Master. She did—once—quickly. Then when Master still didn't turn around, moving farther into the crowd, she barked twice and then twice more. Master still wouldn't turn around.

Now the panic really set in. She was losing ground, and then something hit her in the side and she went flying. When she regained her legs, she realized she was in the path of more feet, more stomping, more kicking. She growled inwardly and barked twice. Still nothing. No Master. Panic...

Master!

It was then that her instincts kicked in. She took the long route around that afforded her the chance to run as fast as her legs would carry her to see Master. Liberty had to see Master. She knew that she would probably outrun him. That was okay. She would meet him on the other side. He would be there, and she would be waiting.

Then another loud noise sounded. It seemed to freeze time for her. She felt everything around her shudder, but she couldn't understand what it had been. To her it was just a loud noise. The cause of the rumble didn't even make her stride falter.

She had one focus: *Master, Master, Master*. Then she saw him.

He glanced to the left and she caught the opening. She saw him with his kind new friend, the one who always gave her food under the table and let her sit on the couch even though she knew Master didn't like that. He would have anger in his eyes at first, then he would do that funny thing with his mouth and his look of happiness would return.

Something smelled wrong. She smelled new things now, bigger smells. She recognized blood, human blood. She couldn't see if it was Master's blood, but it didn't smell like him.

All the smells were jumbled together: dirty floors, bleached bathrooms, metal, blood, more humans....

Master. Liberty smelled him again. At least she knew she was going the right way. She took a hard left, panting, and bolted through a man's legs, getting clipped on the side of her head in the process. She ignored it, moved on, quickly now, dodging legs, ignoring faces and screams.

Smells. Too many smells.

Smells for days.

She couldn't see that she'd made the wide loop around the big room. Then she heard more screaming. Maybe people were screaming at her. Then a lot of people lay down and almost fell on top of her. Liberty slid across the floor, her claws struggling to find a hold, and she bolted over a group of huddling children. She made it around, and there he was—*Master!*

But he was looking the other way. They all were. More men - ones that looked different. They all had those things in their hands, things Liberty knew could make noise that hurt her ears.

A man standing by himself was looking at Master. They were saying things that she didn't understand. Her ears perked up, trying to understand the language, trying to read the faces. She couldn't see Master's face.

Look at me, look at me, Master!

He wouldn't. And then someone near Master rose from the ground. Liberty recognized this was a woman, and then everything went away except for two things: Master: her pulsing beacon in the drowning fog, and the woman who burned red like fire: burning, pain, danger.

Her instincts kicked in. She started toward the woman who was so close now, and she sprang off the back of a man who was lying on the ground, moaning. She flew, teeth bared. *Danger.* She needed to save Master from the danger. *Protect Master.*

She loved him. He loved her. This woman wanted to take that away, and Liberty wouldn't let that happen. *No.*

Her jaws clamped onto the back of the woman's neck. At that moment she heard the familiar sounds of that thing in the man's hand. She couldn't see him, but she felt something tear across the left side of her face. She didn't flinch. She held on for dear life. She held on for Master.

And then she felt something like a punch to her chest. She was flying away. She suddenly felt sad. She couldn't see, but she felt Master nearby. She flew and then she fell. Liberty felt the pain then, the shadows edging in on her vision. She tried to stand and even tried to bark. It was no good. The pain was too much.

Where was Master?

Master?

Then she felt no more as a curtain of black enveloped her.

CHAPTER TWENTY-NINE

When the man with the gun raised his weapon, Cal felt more exposed than ever before in his life. It wasn't himself he was worried about. It was Diane, so he covered her with his body, shielding her from death. As he moved to do so, taking care to stay between her and the bomber that Daniel had described to them, he saw a flash of movement and grasped for recognition. He had wondered where Liberty had gone. He usually never had to worry about her.

Cal had heard Anna scream, and he didn't know why. He was fixated on the bolt of flying fury that was Liberty. Her aim was true, and she took the terrorist on the back of the neck, just as the man with the gun fired three times.

Cal saw one of the rounds hit the would-be bomber in the chest, and then the next exploded through her cheek bone. Then the last, almost dead center in her forehead, going out the back of her skull.

That wasn't all of it: there was another explosion, a bit smaller than the earlier two. This one, which must have been in the girl's backpack, blasted through the girl and must have hit Liberty.

The shock of the blast made Cal flinch. His body had reacted by shutting his eyes for him, and he hadn't seen what had happened to his loyal companion.

He looked now, careful to yell immediately, "Stay down!" to Diane. He ran toward the carnage, ignored the bloody chunks of the terrorist and finally found Liberty ten feet away. She was a bloody heap on the floor. Her eyes were closed, and her tongue hung out of her mouth. Cal bent down. He knew how to save a human life, but he had no idea how to save a dog's. He felt her neck and thought he sensed a faint pulse, but the rest of her sleek coat and entire lower half was drenched in blood. Her side torn open, Cal could see her insides.

"You tried to save me," he whispered, but there was no response. No happy wag of the tail. There was blood, so much blood.

In that moment, their relationship changed. He'd had dogs before, had gladly taken Liberty in, if only because she was a happy reminder of his cousin, Travis Hayden. Most days, Cal called her Travis's dog. Now, as Cal's hands struggled to push her organs back into her body, she became his dog. He tore off his shirt and wrapped it around her tightly, but still the blood came. He picked her up, her body somehow feeling ten pounds lighter than it had.

When he turned, he saw that the French police had tackled the man with the gun. The man who had shot the terrorist, the man who Cal thought would shoot them. There was no time to think about that now. He wasn't focused, as more people rushed to leave the battered train station. Cal rejoined his friends.

"We need to get to the hospital."

"Oh my God, Cal," Diane said, holding Liberty's head.

"Come on, follow me," Daniel ordered. Cal noticed that Anna's face had gone stark white, then he remembered the scream. She had been screaming at the man with the gun, but that didn't matter now. He only had one focus: getting Liberty and the others out safe. So off they ran, four more people rushing from the scene of the attack.

* * *

ROURKE GLANCED down as the handcuffs were jammed onto his wrists. One of the idiot cops had shot him. His leg burned.

"Take it easy!" Rourke said through gritted teeth. The French police screamed at him more in French. He wished they'd speak English, or that Maurice would come back and explain things to them, but no.

Rourke realized that Maurice and his men were probably long gone. Maybe it was better that way. They had handcuffed him, and then there were multiple phones in Rourke's face. They were taking pictures. He couldn't believe it. The cops were actually taking pictures of him as if he were a celebrity. Then he saw the familiar black hair. Anna had gotten away; he'd saved her. Three shots were all it took. It had been instinctual to protect his former charge, his body reacted quicker than his mind.

Rourke had only been in one shootout his entire career and that had been a mistake. Wrong place at the wrong time, the rookie FBI agent thrown into the big leagues too soon. He'd lost his veteran partner that day. He had died in part because Rourke had missed every shot, and from that day on he vowed that would never happen again. So, he'd spent countless hours at the range, paying for special courses out of his own pocket and went to Arizona, Tennessee, and Texas for specialized weapons training. It looked like those thousands of trigger pulls had paid off.

He knew his shots had killed the terrorist. There was no

use going for the hand at that distance, so he'd aimed for the head on his second and third shots. He had been satisfied to see the bomber go down, and then the explosion finished the rest. Rourke had flinched with the rest of them, thinking that he'd failed in the end. When he lifted his eyes, he was still standing, the real terrorist wasn't. The woman was no more than two bloody chunks on the ground.

"Get on your feet!" the other cop said.

"I can't. You shot me in the leg," Rourke sent back. The knee in his back dug in further, stealing Rourke's breath.

"Where are the others?" The cop asked, and that's when Rourke realized that they thought he was part of the plot. He, Ian Rourke, the patriotic American who had spent his life defending the Constitution and seeing that bad men got their due, was now the suspect in a terrorist plot. Maybe it was because he knew that Anna was safe for the time being, or maybe it was the absurdity of the entire situation that they thought he, a light-skinned American, was part of the bomb plot. Rourke laughed, the sound coming out as a cough, and then he couldn't contain the maniacal mirth boiling over as if he hadn't laughed in years.

The police stepped back, as if the laughter was some precursor to another detonation and that only made Rourke laugh louder. They stared at him, the sound itself building, and suddenly they must have decided it was enough. They dragged him to his feet, his right leg useless. As he tried to support his own weight, they must have seen it, because one officer grabbed each arm and dragged him from the train station, away from the death, leaving the carnage behind. All the while, Ian Rourke laughed at the alternate reality.

CHAPTER THIRTY

For the next two days, Paris was on lock-down. The Gare du Nord station was only one location of nine where simultaneous explosions took place. Yet another off-shoot of Al-Qaeda was taking responsibility for the attacks, proudly proclaiming on the internet that they'd struck another savage blow into the heart of the enemy. Many of the places Cal and Diane had visited earlier on their holiday had been left in shambles.

The Eiffel Tower was closed: it had been slightly damaged in the attacks, and the French police and military were using it as a vantage point: posting snipers, setting up communications, and generally keeping an eye on the populace.

In this beautiful city that boasted of its openness, martial law now reigned. A city-wide curfew had been enacted and all tourist stops had been closed until the investigation was complete. As is so often the case, deaths now numbered in the thousands.

Injuries, which numbered eight times as many as casualties were soon punctuated by stories of heroism, love and valor. There'd been a father of three from Estonia, who was looking for his children and wife near Notre Dame and he had gotten lost getting off the train. In all the confusion of the morning commuters, he had gone the wrong way and incredibly stumbled on one of the attackers, a young man in his early twenties preparing to carry out his heinous act.

CCTV and personal cell phones wielded by video-happy tourists picked up the entire scene where the burly Estonian had literally picked up the terrorist and thrown him into the Seine. The gasps and awe of the crowd were captured on numerous cameras as the body of the terrorist and his weapons fell into the water. An explosion rocked the area but no one had been harmed, except the terrorist.

Then, there was the group of policemen who had foiled the getaway of a trio of terrorists who had either lost their nerve or had been ordered to go back.

The most curious story of all came from one of the busiest train stations in Paris. There, of all things, a dog had become a national hero. This was no military-trained Belgian Malinois or a dog used for guard duty. It was first reported by a local police station, but despite the grainy footage of the animal, it was identified as a German Shorthaired Pointer, a popular hunting dog. It was likely someone's pet. The video being shared across France showed the dog clearly jumping off a man's back and attacking the train station bomber, biting the back of her neck.

One second later, one of the explosives in the terrorist's backpack went off, flinging the dog away, sealing the terrorist's fate. The Paris police were surprised at the questions about the dog from the incident at the Gare du Nord. News people wanted to know who the dog was, who did it belong to, and how many people had it saved? The police later determined that only one handful of the charges had gone off in that backpack; the others had malfunctioned and somehow did not ignite the others. The largest weapons were in the rolling case on the ground and didn't detonate either. But at the time, it seemed that this dog, someone's loyal companion, saved the day.

Word traveled fast concerning the dog's fate. By the time Cal and the others had reached the hospital, one of the doctors, who had seen the first video of the dog, had readily taken in the new patient. It was another stroke of luck that the French doctor had grown up on a farm miles outside of Paris, his father a veterinarian. The doctor himself had once wanted to be an animal physician. Fate had turned him in a different direction, but he was familiar with the dog's anatomy. He could only attempt to put Liberty back together. When he emerged after surgery, his tone was solemn but optimistic.

"She lost a great deal of blood, and I had to remove parts of her intestine, but I believe she will heal. Now, if you'll excuse me, I have other patients that require my attention." He marched off before Cal could offer his gratitude. Diane gave him a small hug.

Daniel and Anna had gone to find a place to stay, so it was just the two of them in a private waiting area that served VIPs. They'd been met there by a nurse who had come to fetch them from the crowded waiting room. It was all so crazy. Their vacation had been turned upside down, and now here they were in a Paris hospital, not because one of them had been injured, but because a dog - a dog! - had been injured.

Cal shook his head. "Am I being stupid for being so emotional about this?"

"No," Diane said, "She's part of you now. She's your family."

Cal just nodded. He knew she was right. He'd just gone through the motions before. When Daniel presented Liberty to him, she had attached herself to Cal right away, but the feeling hadn't necessarily been mutual. She was obedient and loving, but Cal had seen it as more of a promise to his dead cousin that he would care for her, see to her well-being, but nothing else. Now something had changed, but Cal couldn't let that stop him from getting things done. During those two days, Cal constantly traveled back and forth between a nearby three-bedroom flat Anna had procured through her corporation, and the hospital.

After settling in at the apartment, Cal and Daniel tried to come up with a game plan. If getting out of Paris had been important before the attacks, now it was imperative. While their faces hadn't been shown on national television, police had gladly displayed the face of the man with the gun, and when Cal first arrived at the apartment he'd asked Anna about the man.

"You know him, don't you?"

"I did know him," Anna said.

She explained her connection with Ian Rourke, that he'd been with the FBI tasked with facilitating the relationship between the American government and The Pension.

"But the last I heard, he'd left the Bureau to start his own firm or work freelance. I now know that was him when we ran from the hotel that night. He was there, across the street, in the open doorway, hiding in the shadows. I just caught a glimpse of him, but now I know for sure."

A quick internet search of the man produced nothing. If Neil were with them in Paris, he could have found the information they needed. But he wasn't. He was in Vienna with Doc and Jonas. The four of them were trapped, for the time being, without a way home, and without a way to find their friends. But as Cal waited, and as he stroked Liberty's head, he promised that he would find this Ian Rourke and finally get to the truth of who was behind it all.

CHAPTER THIRTY-ONE

The concern on Congressman McKnight's face as he watched the Paris updates unfold wasn't the same as that on the faces of the staffers around him. They watched in horror as images of bloody travelers blasted their way across the Atlantic. There were endless shots of body bags waiting to travel to their final destinations. There was evidence on an hourly loop now, a video of the man currently in police custody, who the Paris authorities believed might have been part of the terrorist plot.

Congressman McKnight had recognized the face immediately. Ian Rourke was in the middle of that mess, and with a gun no less. Of course, McKnight didn't know the whole story, only that released to the public, but he knew enough. He knew when a relationship was worth salvaging, but there was still something he needed from this one, something that Rourke had in his possession at the time of the attacks somewhere in Paris. He needed it to take him down — Brandon Zimmer, the key to the White House. But McKnight had to be careful. There was no one he could discuss this with, but he was used to that.

First, no one could know of his connection to Rourke. That could lead to his undoing. Second, he needed to get his hands on the information Rourke had stolen from The Jefferson Group. And third, Rourke needed to disappear. He'd done his job initially, but now the former FBI agent was damaged goods, a liability. As a candidate for the presidency, McKnight couldn't have liabilities on his side, only assets.

He made a phone call to the chairman of the Republican National Convention. The former senator apologized profusely and stated that if he had known that Rourke could have been caught up in such a drama, he never would have recommended him to McKnight.

McKnight had tried, said it wasn't the man's fault, these things happen. But now, the trash needed to be taken out. The chairman understood completely and said that it would be arranged. McKnight would have no further contact with Ian Rourke, and Rourke would never have the opportunity to implicate McKnight.

So for the moment, the presidential candidate from Miami, Florida was appeased. He had a busy schedule after all. America wanted him to outline his plan to root out terrorists worldwide. They wanted to prevent something like Paris happening in New York City, Chicago, or maybe even L.A. His people needed him now. They needed him to be strong; they needed him to be the face of confidence and provide an image of resolute determination. So, he put on yet another mask to give the public what they wanted, what they needed and what they deserved.

CHAPTER THIRTY-TWO

Hours later, while smoking another cigarette, Maurice stood outside the Paris safe house, mulling over the day's proceedings. The day before, the day of the attacks, was a jumble of confusion. It wasn't that he had been surprised by the attacks. Paris had been waiting ever since the earlier smaller assaults.

This had been France's 9/11. The idiots in the government would finally come to understand that all the enlightenment in the world couldn't battle these terrorists. Maurice has been on the front lines as a contractor both in Iraq and Afghanistan. He had snuck across the border in Pakistan and gladly taken the lives of terrorists, and he was good at that. But then, with the election of a new president, the French resolve had wilted away. That left Maurice without a job, scrounging to make rent, and begging old friends to take him in.

But he'd missed the gravy train. While his peers in the military had gone out one-by-one to get jobs in the private sector, he'd stayed on, believing in the French message. Even if he was just a simple contractor receiving government pay, he still felt like he could have been one of the millions under Napoleon's command. Therefore, he'd fallen in with contractors from other countries, most recently the Americans. It was good money, and they needed an experienced man who understood the French way of doing things.

He'd gladly taken a contract with Ian Rourke. Everything had gone well until that incident at the hotel where Maurice had taken it upon himself to be a little more proactive. He'd seen what the two men in the hotel room were capable of when they took out five highly trained men, including himself. For being bested Maurice was ashamed, but he wasn't ashamed of what he had done.

After receiving that berating by Rourke, Maurice felt no love for the Americans. He respected them, of course. What military man couldn't respect the might of the United States' sheer power that their aircraft carriers could bring to the region, or the lethal capacity of their Special Operations troops.

But in Maurice's opinion, he and Rourke were small potatoes. In Maurice's eyes, he should have had command of the entire operation. After the incident in the train station, he had fled and was now holed up inside the safe house. Maurice had thought that maybe it was for the best; it was time to cut ties with the Americans.

The entire operation was ruined because some goddamned Middle Easterners had wanted to blow themselves up and take Parisians with them. But then, the call had come, and the words on the other end made Maurice smile. His wish had been granted.

The rest of Rourke's Americans were to be interrogated. Maurice had called in a few friends whom he knew were liberal performing their interrogations. One of them had to know where Rourke's prized catch was. They'd searched the entire safe house and hadn't found the laptop that contained the information his employer needed. After hearing the dollar amount clearly over the phone, Maurice knew he would pull out all the stops to find the treasured package. But after hours of searching, he needed more time spent interrogating the Americans to be closer to finding the prize.

Maurice flicked his spent cigarette to the ground and tapped a new one from the pack in his pocket. Rourke was the key, of course, but he was being held in an undisclosed location. The foolish Paris police still believed that he had been part of the terrorist plot. Maurice knew better. A friend on the force told him that Rourke had actually shot the last terrorist, so it was really all just a misunderstanding. Some cruel joke dropped on the head of Ian Rourke, but it worked perfectly for Maurice.

The Frenchman would be well paid for his exploits, but only after he obtained what the American employer wanted. This meant Maurice and his men had to get to Rourke. That had been part of the plan and part of the demand made by the American. Thus, Maurice would have to figure out a way in; it was something he always did. It was good to have friends in Paris, especially friends with a strong sense of French pride. They believed that everything should be done to secure the motherland. Maurice raised his hand and drew an invisible cross-hair in the air, imagining Rourke's face in front of it. "I'm coming for you, my friend," Maurice whispered. He then smiled and took another lung-filling drag from his cigarette.

CHAPTER THIRTY-THREE

Anna couldn't help but think maybe she could've prevented all this. Not the terrorist attacks, of course, but if she'd remembered that it was Rourke. She could've recognized him outside the hotel. The others might've been able to do something. She didn't know exactly what Cal did for a living, but she could tell, by the respect Daniel showed him, Cal was someone important and that he had means. Maybe he could've done something if he'd had the information.

Now, the world was in shambles. Paris had been rocked by the attacks. She loved Paris, and she knew its people would rise from the rubble. But it still pained her to see the funeral processions and the armed men walking the streets where tourists had gathered just days before.

The only TV in the rented flat was on day and night. Cal and Daniel took turns keeping watch. Anna tried to match her schedule with Daniel's, engaging him in light conversation whenever possible. But she felt the heavy burden of knowing that Rourke might've been behind Daniel's problems. This burden made her exhausted in a way she hadn't known in years. She knew she was suffering from deep depression. It was something that both her mother and father had struggled with, even in their twenties, and now it seemed history would repeat itself.

Anna, of course, had the means to see the best doctors. She also practiced meditation, allowing her to analyze situations dispassionately. Now she took control, quietly focusing on her breathing. She sat cross-legged on her bed, willing the ill thoughts to fly away from her mind.

She was just arriving at a place of needed peace when there was a knock at the apartment door – loud and anonymous. It made her body tense. Anna and Diane were sharing the room, so she looked to Diane's bed. Diane was gone, but then Anna heard the shower running and realized that Diane must be inside.

Anna leapt from the bed, sliding into the living room fast enough to see Daniel and Cal position themselves with their backs to the wall on either side of the front door. Daniel saw her and motioned to her to stay clear.

"Who is it?" Cal asked through the door.

"Delivery," came a man's voice.

"Sorry, you must have the wrong apartment. We didn't order anything," Cal said calmly, but Anna could see his body was prepared to strike. It was then that she noticed that both Cal and Daniel held knives in their hands.

"A mutual friend put in the order," the voice said. The person still sounded congenial, but you could tell the person wasn't going away.

Cal and Daniel looked at each other. Then they looked to Anna, who just shrugged. "Which friend?" Cal asked.

"Andy."

Anna didn't know who Andy was, but the two men protecting the door exchanged another glance, this time, hopeful. Cal didn't relax, but he did ease the door open.

A dark red bag appeared in the doorway, and that was all that Anna could see. She instantly recognized the logo of Cartier.

"May I come in?" the stranger's voice asked.

Cal grabbed the bag and stepped back, allowing Daniel to open the door the rest of the way. The man's face was somehow familiar, the type of face you see on Spanish telenovelas or in London's gossip pages. The suit was impeccably tailored. The carnation in his left breast pocket was a strange choice, but it went along with Anna's snap judgement of the man. He was very sure of himself, flamboyant and cocky. The man walked into the room, and Daniel closed the door behind him. After locking the door, Daniel did not hesitate to frisk the man for weapons.

"What's in the bag?" Cal asked, his eyes still trained on the newcomer.

"Have a look for yourself," said the man, wholly unimpressed.

Daniel finished searching him from head to toe, and he now looked inside the bag, then back up to the stranger. "Are those jewelry boxes?"

The man nodded. "One each for the ladies. I picked them out myself. Beautiful diamond bracelets of the highest quality. *Your* gift is under boxes."

Cal lifted two red boxes out of the bag and set them on the coffee table. When he looked inside again, his eyebrows rose. Anna thought she caught the hint of a smile. "How did you say you know Andy?" Cal asked.

"I didn't, but if you ask me nicely, I'd be happy to tell you."

Cal's hand came out of the bag holding a black pistol. "Forty five?"

The stranger nodded. Cal placed the pistol next to the twin red boxes on the table, and he extracted three more identical weapons, along with brown boxes that must've contained the ammunition and magazines for them.

"Have a seat," Cal said after Daniel finished his inspection. The man nodded his thanks, and took a seat fluidly, crossing one leg over the other, completely relaxed in the tense surroundings. While Cal still scrutinized the man, Daniel had relaxed as well. He was now standing off to the side with a look of amusement stamped on his normally placid features.

"While I appreciate the gifts, it still doesn't explain how you know Andy or why he sent you." The man nodded, as if he'd been expecting the observation. "If you don't mind, you should probably start at the beginning."

"My name is Maximilian Frazier. I am a citizen of Austria and a resident of Vienna."

Vienna? Anna thought. Hadn't Daniel said something about friends in Vienna?

"Your friend Andy has been trying to recruit me for some time. I was, how should I put this, otherwise engaged in Austria's affairs of state. We may not be as mighty as you Americans, but we have developed a respectable intelligence service, of which I am a proud member. And thus, as a loyal servant to my government, I am now at your disposal."

"Wait, you said Andy was trying to recruit you—recruit you for what?"

"That's a long story, and it's probably best if I let your friend tell you details. Suffice it to say we're working together now, and when he found out that I was in contact with Jonas, he ..."

"Wait, you know where Jonas is?" Cal interrupted. Frazier gave Cal a look as if he didn't like to be interrupted. Anna quickly realized he was just teasing, a smile now erupting on his face.

"Jonas and I are old friends. And yes, I have seen him,

Neil and Dr. Higgins. They are safe, and they will be here soon. It was necessary to take a more secretive route, given the current situation in Paris."

"And what about the others, our friends in Amsterdam?"

"I'm afraid I don't have any information for you there, but I am prepared to get you out of France and back to the United States."

"We can't do that yet," Cal said, now pacing back-and-forth. "Are you sure Andy didn't say anything about Amsterdam?"

Max shook his head. "No, but you can ask him, if you'd like," Frazier fished a phone out of his suit pocket and handed it to Cal. "He's waiting for your call."

During the phone call, Anna whispered in Daniel's ear, "Who is Andy?"

"Major Bartholomew Andrews. He goes by Andy, and he was Cal's platoon commander in the Marines. He's a good guy who now works for the CIA."

When Cal hung up, Anna could see relief on Cal's face. "Andy said Top and Gaucho are on the other side of town - that they've been here for a day."

"Well, that's good news," Daniel said. "Did he say anything about our friend in Washington?"

Cal shook his head. "He said he would be able to talk when we got home, and I think he's right. But listen, I don't think we should leave until we've got this Rourke guy figured out. He knows something, and we need to find out what information he possesses."

Daniel nodded in agreement. "Mr. Frazier, do you have any contacts in the DGSI?" Daniel asked.

Anna knew that DGSI stood for General Directorate for Internal Security, a fact her grandfather had once relayed on a trip to Lyon.

"A few," Frazier answered. "Why do you ask?"

"They have a man in custody, a man they believe is behind the terrorist attacks, or is at least an accomplice. We, or Anna," Daniel said, pointing to her, "thinks that there has to be something else."

"Do you need information, or ...."

"We need to talk to him," Cal finished. "But, we need to do it soon."

Frazier crossed his arms over his chest, thinking, "That could be tricky, but I'll see what I can do. Now, in the meantime, I suggest that the four of you," then he pointed at Liberty who hadn't left Cal's side. "Correction, the five of you should get some rest. As our mutual friend, Jonas, used to tell me after returning home at eight o'clock in the morning from the discos, 'You look like crap.'"

CHAPTER THIRTY-FOUR

Maurice could barely contain himself. He almost felt sorry for the French police who'd been holding Rourke. They had seen Rourke as their prize. Maurice recognized more than one face that had already graced the television screens. Each officer wanted to be one of the personalities to get credit for taking down Rourke, thus keeping a key part of the terrorist plot from fruition.

However, a few phone calls to Maurice's American employer and the French plan had changed. Maurice walked out of the government building, one hand on the hooded figure of Ian Rourke, the other fingering an automatic weapon. He was surrounded by his own men, gathered for protection and what lay ahead.

They weren't afraid of dirty work. They liked it almost as much as Maurice. Yes, what would come next would be fun. That day would be enjoyable, and it would be especially rewarding in this case.

Maurice usually excelled at prying information from the tight lips of his captives. The Afghan chieftains had always been tight-lipped, and Maurice was more than willing to call their bluff. All it only took was to kill a handful of the chieftain's family members in front of them before information was gleaned. He couldn't do that with Rourke, of course, because Rourke was a bachelor. He reeked of it, all work and no play. He was a serious American who always did his job, sticking to the rules. It had chafed Maurice from the day of their first meeting, but he'd gone along with it, sensing a greater opportunity would one day present itself.

While they piled into the windowless white panel van at the curb, and Maurice's entourage scanned the streets, Maurice bent closer to Rourke's ear and said, "I look forward to talking with you my friend and, might I just add, your life depends on it." He shoved Rourke hard in the back, causing his captive to slam against the far wall of the van. Maurice just chuckled to his men, slid into the seat and closed the door shut. It was his first act as the new master, and Maurice relished the feeling.

CHAPTER THIRTY-FIVE

True to his word, Max Frazier V and company had arrived in Paris. Dr. Higgins looked like he was taking it all in stride. Jonas looked disheveled, like a man who was having his first operational experience, but Cal was most surprised to see the change that had come over Neil Patel.

Neil and Cal had been friends for a long time, since their time spent at the University of Virginia. Since then, Neil had been through a lot. He had lost his parents. He'd conquered drug abuse, been kidnapped and lost a foot, but he'd made it through. Yet, there was something different about Neil now. That happy cockiness he was famous for was no longer present. Instead, from across the room, Neil now looked like a defeated man. Cal wanted to set his friend back on the right path.

"I really messed up this time, Cal," Neil said, his whole body shaking. "You are always telling me to be careful, and I really thought I had been, but now this happens, and I placed all of you in danger. I don't know ..."

Cal put a hand on his friend's shaking shoulder. "It's not your fault, Neil," remarked Cal, his words true.

His eyes blinking, as if Neil was grasping at his last hope, he responded, "but it is. They got in. They must know about who we are, and who we've been working for."

"I hate to tell you this, buddy, but no system is airtight. We all messed up, and now it's time to put the pieces back together, but I need your help. We can't do this without you, and I want you to stay here. Take a nap if you need to. Take a shower. We'll be waiting in the next room. There's no rush. When you come out there, I need your A-Game. I need the Neil Patel who doesn't know how to lose. I need the Neil Patel who could make a rocket ship out of a pen and a stick of gum."

Neil nodded. He did not look up this time when he said, "I'd probably need a couple more things than just a pen and gum, you know?" He looked up and there was that familiar twinkle in Neil's eye. It was a start. Neil wasn't all the way back. It was too soon for that, but Cal prayed that his friend would return.

He patted Neil one more time on the shoulder, then left him to decompress in a well-needed shower. When Cal emerged from the bedroom, Jonas was in the middle of retelling their tale of their escape from Vienna. They'd taken a helicopter to get to the airport and boarded a private jet. On the way to Paris, they had been diverted because of the attacks.

"It really felt like a scene out of *Planes, Trains, and Automobiles*," Jonas said, laughing. "But with Max's help, we got here, and I can honestly say it's good to see you guys," then he noticed that Cal had returned to the room.

"How's Neil?"

"He'll be fine," Cal said. "Has he been like this the whole time?"

Jonas nodded, "He thinks it's his fault, but it's not."

"I told him the same thing," said Cal. "I think he needs

what we all need - something to do. Max, I was wondering if I could get your help with something,"

"How can I help?" Max asked. Cal told him what he had in mind. When he was finished, Max nodded and said, "Let me make a few calls. I don't think it'll be a problem."

When Neil emerged from the shower, he felt closer to being whole again. He knew the shower helped, but it was really Cal's words of reassurance that bolstered his confidence. There'd been plenty to be worried about on the trip from Vienna, but what had really wreaked havoc on Neil's nerves was the thought of confronting Cal, of telling him what he had done. He didn't want to let his old friend down, especially after all the warnings and suggestions that maybe he shouldn't push the envelope too much.

As he'd soaked blissfully under the hot shower water, Neil realized that he was no different than the gun-toting operators of The Jefferson Group, escaping boundaries in their own ways, and Neil escaping in his. When you did that for a living, it was only inevitable that something would go wrong at some point.

What had the others done? They hadn't dropped to their knees and given up. No, with their limited resources, they stood tall and attempted to fix it. As Neil toweled himself off, he made a choice. He would fix it. When he emerged into the spacious living area, he felt like a new man.

"Did you leave me any hot water?" Jonas asked.

Neil shrugged. "Maybe," and he let out a chuckle. "Man, I needed that. Next order of business is getting some new clothes or at least getting these washed," Neil said.

"The girls are on it," Daniel offered.

"The girls?" Neil asked. Neil suddenly remembered that Diane was supposed to be with them.

"Yeah, Diane and ... well, Daniel's new friend," Cal said, slyly. The newcomers all looked at Daniel, who just stood there, stone-faced. "Her name is Anna, and she's a very nice girl, right Daniel?" Cal needled.

Daniel nodded without uttering a word. The rest of them just kind of pretended not to stare. *Daniel, with a girl?* Neil thought. He fought to save his friend from the embarrassment and asked where Max had gone. Then the front door opened revealing Max with a large cardboard box in his arms.

"I have a surprise for all of you," Max said to the room. But first, he walked over to Neil and offered him the box. "And, this is for you, my friend. You can't keep it, but feel free to use it during your stay in Paris."

Neil didn't bother going to the dining room table. He just dropped to the ground and started tearing open the box like a child at Christmas. It could only be one thing, and he was right. When he pulled the black loaner computer out of the box, Neil read the blue sticker that read in French, "Property of the French Government."

On a yellow sticky note were a list of passwords, and when he opened the laptop he saw that there was a browser already prepared. When he clicked through each tab, a different login screen greeted him.

Neil smiled, "I don't know how you got your hands on this, Max, but thanks."

Max nodded, and then bowed. "Now, if you'll humor me, your next surprise should be coming in ..." Max looked at his watch and held up his fingers, "Five, four, three, two..."

"Can someone tell me how to get a decent cup of coffee around here?" boomed a familiar voice from the open doorway. A moment later, Master Sargent Willy Trent stepped in followed by a pretty brunette who nodded shyly to the men in the room.

"Boys, this is Lydia. Lydia, these are the boys." She waved at the room and sidled up next to Top.

"Where's Gaucho?" Cal asked.

"Did somebody say my name?" Gaucho walked into the room, a huge smile on his face. "I never thought I'd be so happy to see your ugly faces," Gaucho said. There were hugs all around.

Relief in the room was palpable, but it was cut short by an announcement from Max. "I hate to be the bearer of bad news during this glorious reunion, but my local contacts have just informed me that your Mr. Rourke has just been released into United States custody."

"Who's Rourke?" Top asked.

"Yeah, somebody's going to have to give me the Cliff Notes version of what the hell's going on," Gaucho said.

"I don't get it," Cal said. "Was Andy behind this, too?"

Max shook his head. "He didn't say anything about getting Rourke released."

"Yeah, but he did find us," Top offered.

"I can see from the looks in the room that that's a story for another day. Here's the strange thing...." Max continued, "the authority was given by the American government but the men sent in to get Rourke were French nationals."

"That doesn't make any sense. Did he say where they were taking him?"

Max shook his head. "My contact says they've got their hands full with more leads linked to the terrorists. Other than Rourke's illegal possession of the firearm, I think the police and even the government figured out he wasn't part of the plot. He turned out to be too much trouble, more trouble than he was worth."

"Wait, so who is this Rourke guy?" Gaucho asked.

"We think he's the one behind everything," Daniel answered.

"Well, at least he's the one who did everything," Cal clarified. "We still don't know who's behind it."

Gaucho coughed out a laugh, "Here and I thought you guys would have all the answers."

"I've got an idea," Neil said. All eyes were on him now, and he keenly felt the scrutiny, so he focused on what was familiar: the laptop sitting in front of him. He clicked through the few screens and found what he was looking for. "Max, when did you say the French nationals took him?"

"Ten, maybe fifteen minutes ago," Max said.

Neil nodded. He was moving faster now, the rhythm coming back to him. "If I can only," he muttered. "Yes, there it is."

"Do you want to tell us what's going on?" Cal asked.

"I can find him, Cal. Actually, I did find him."

"Find who?"

"Rourke, isn't that who we need?"

Cal looked confused. Then Neil lifted up the laptop and turned it so the others could see the screen. There, in full color, high definition was the man from the train station. The video showed Ian Rourke being handcuffed and then led to the exit by men dressed in black. Rourke was led out to the street after the men placed a hood over his head.

"Ladies and gentlemen, it's show time," Top said.

CHAPTER THIRTY-SIX

McKnight's "campaign face," as he liked to call it, dropped as soon as he slipped into the car. The head of the RNC handed him a bottle of water and asked, "How did it go?"

"How do they all go?" McKnight said. "Just another stop and it will all be over soon."

"Look, Tony, I don't know exactly what you had Rourke doing in Paris, but maybe if you could tell me, I can be of some assistance."

McKnight shook his head, cracked open the bottled water and chugged half of it before answering. "It's better if you don't know, at least for now. Call it plausible deniability, but you'll find out; don't worry. Speaking of Rourke, is he in our custody?"

The former senator from Wisconsin nodded. "I just got word that they're taking him to a safe location." McKnight almost winced from the feeling of relief. Rourke was the key, and now they had him.

"And the information?" McKnight asked.

"The Frenchman says they are working on it."

"Did you say the Frenchman?" McKnight asked incredulously. "I thought you had an ex-CIA or FBI guy taking care of this."

McKnight's companion shook his head. "This was the best we could do. He was a contractor working for Rourke, but I'm told he's very motivated to accomplish this mission."

"Meaning you offered him a lot of money," McKnight guessed. The senator nodded. "Is there any way that this Frenchman can trace Rourke back to me?"

"No...." the senator answered with a total lack of confidence.

"Not unless Rourke says something," McKnight finished for him. McKnight was beginning to feel a familiar stab of pain in his head. "Make sure this Frenchman sticks to the script. The data I need could be on a laptop, a memory card —something small and portable. Tell him to find that, get rid of Rourke and we'll double his fee."

To his credit, the senator didn't flinch even though, technically, he was paying the bill. *Yet another perk of being a presidential candidate*, McKnight thought. *Someone else picks up the dinner tab*.

"Oh, and senator? I know I don't have to tell you this, but I want to make sure we're on the same page."

"You won't offend me, Tony. Say what you're thinking."

McKnight appreciated the man's openness to critique. For the first time, he looked at the Wisconsin senator in a different light. He'd been a powerful man in the Senate, but he had given it all up because of some family emergency. He'd been called back into service for the struggling Republican party, and he had done a masterful job of restructuring the party's image. McKnight knew that maybe in another time, the senator from Wisconsin could become president.

But now was McKnight's time. A man from Florida, a congressman who would bring back the Hispanic vote. His idle thoughts drifted away and then he turned to the window watching the world pass by.

"Just make sure I get that information."

"I'll take care of it."

"Oh and senator? Make sure you buckle up, it's about to be a wild October ride."

CHAPTER THIRTY-SEVEN

"They shut down your company, you know."

Rourke wasn't surprised. The French police had only been too happy to show him the news coverage. As he watched from the cell, he saw his face accompanying the faces of the dead bombers, and he knew someone back home would start the compartmentalization process.

What he had been surprised about was the speed with which McKnight or one of his lackeys had snatched him from the Paris jail. He'd been slightly uncomfortable there, but at least he had been safe. Rourke knew the whole time that somebody would come. He imagined a platoon of lawyers from the State Department, or even American Federal Marshals.

But who, of all people, had shown up? That goddamned Maurice.

Rourke truly hated the man, and that anger fueled him. It cleared his tired mind, allowing him to focus on his surroundings. They'd put a hood over his head at the police station, and then they'd boarded a vehicle with leather seats. Not a word was said as they drove, and Rourke focused on measuring the time. He wasn't that precise, but he was close. Thirty minutes later, he estimated, the car doors opened. He was yanked from the vehicle, dragged up one flight of stairs and then another. He wished the hood wasn't on so he could at least smell whether he was in an industrial warehouse or apartment. However, they'd left the hood on for the duration of the journey and even after they'd strapped him to the hard-backed chair.

There were murmured conversations all around him, but they were in French. Even though Rourke strained to hear, he couldn't understand what the men were saying. He did recognize Maurice's voice; the man was obviously in charge.

While a part of him monitored the room waiting for a blow to the head or the torso, he tried to imagine what Congressman McKnight was thinking. Unfortunately, there hadn't been time before the attacks at the train station to complete his mission. Now the information was out there, although he was the only man who knew the location of the material McKnight had requested.

That's what McKnight wanted – the final killing blow that would puncture the president's center. Zimmer had gone outside his constitutionally-given rights as chief executive.

The first blow came to the meaty part of Rourke's arm. It didn't hurt as much as it surprised him.

"I can help you, you know." Maurice said, his voice shifting from Rourke's left to his right. Another hit in the other arm. "Your former employer wants one thing. If we can give it to him, all will be forgiven." Rourke just let the man talk. Either the man was lying, or somebody stateside had fed him a line. If Maurice actually believed it, well, he was an even bigger idiot than Rourke had surmised.

Then in a bright flash of light, the hood was gone. Rourke squinted. He and Maurice were the only men in the room. Rourke swiveled his head to survey a room with floor-to-ceiling glass windows and carpeted floors. However, the only furniture in the room, he was currently sitting on. Maurice slapped Rourke's left cheek.

"Don't look around please; look at me." Maurice ordered, grinning, rubbing his knuckles. "The information—I need it. With it I might be able to convince them to let you live. Come Ian, let us work together again. I will even give you some of the money they have promised me and with those funds maybe you can start a new life. I can help you start a new life."

"Go to hell," Rourke said.

Maurice froze, his eyes turning to slits of black. "You would do well to remember that I am the one in charge now. The Americans know that, so it is only natural that you should know that." The Frenchman slid a six-inch blade from his tactical vest. His eyes returned to their normal size, and he stroked the blade lovingly. "You are right-handed, no?" Rourke didn't answer.

"Hold out your right hand," Maurice said conversationally. Rourke ignored him. "Hold out your right hand!" Maurice screamed. Still, Rourke ignored him. "If you do not listen to me..."

"I'm handcuffed to the chair, you idiot!"

"Ah, c'est bon," Maurice remembered. Either the Frenchman hadn't thought things out thoroughly, or he truly was an idiot. "Your leg will do."

Without warning, Maurice struck, plunging the blade into Rourke's thigh, sending shockwaves of pain through his body. He grimaced and tried to hold back the scream, but a pitiful sound escaped his lips. Rourke expected Maurice to extract the blade, but instead he left it there. Rourke stared at it through pain-filled eyes, willing the blade to go away, mentally trying to push it from his throbbing leg.

Maurice must have seen him staring at it, and he grabbed

the hilt and started twisting. It was like nothing Rourke had ever felt before in his lifetime. The steel must have punctured numerous nerves and it probably hit bone.

"Tell me where you put the information," Maurice said calmly, twisting the blade ever so slightly. But to Rourke it felt like three more knives had punctured him. He gritted his teeth and tried to see through the pain. He tried to meet Maurice's eyes, but the tears had made everything blurry.

Then it was gone—at least the blade. The intense pain was still there, but at least the twisting metal was back in Maurice's hand. Dripping with Rourke's blood, Maurice wiped the blade on the back of his shirtsleeve, ensuring that every drop was gone before he spoke.

"This is what you came here to do, Ian. Your mission was to present your employer with certain information. It is only right we provide that information and that you do that for which you were hired. So, come, let us end these silly games. Tell me where it is, and I will have one of my men tend to your wound."

That's when Rourke saw it in the man's eyes. It was the calm of someone who had done this before. Rourke was no interrogator. He'd never felt the need to slap a witness around or threaten them with violence.

But Maurice had seen things. He had done things, and based on the look in his eyes, Rourke knew that using any technique available, Maurice would get the information. He would pry it out using any means necessary and as quickly as possible. What Rourke had to determine was how long he could last through the torture and interrogation. He had to figure out how long he could stretch out the blood bath without breaking.

CHAPTER THIRTY-EIGHT

Max Frazier was full of surprises. Not only had he supplied Neil with a laptop that had access to everything from international crime databases to the best facial recognition software, but he'd also been able to gain access to Paris's entire grid of surveillance cameras, including private cameras all over the city.

Thus, it had been easy for Neil to track this Rourke character and, as the caravan passed through Paris, Neil dissected the lives of each of the men accompanying the hooded figure.

The supposed leader, a man named Maurice, was a well-known military and security contractor. His record looked sterling compared to the rest, who were a collection of hooligans, thugs and suspected rapists. In a word, they were violent men. More than one were wanted by the French police on open warrants.

Neil wondered what the policemen would think if they knew they had released Rourke into these men's hands. They didn't do so with full knowledge, of course. The French had believed the authorization sent by the government that was requested by someone across the Atlantic.

Neil was still trying to piece together who had requested the authorization, but he was getting nowhere. Meanwhile he primarily focused on tracking Rourke and trying to pinpoint exactly where they were heading with him.

The fear was that they would leave Paris; then he'd have to get creative. But they hadn't left Paris. When the caravan did finally stop, it was outside a five-story office building. A quick search revealed the entire second floor was vacant. It was nighttime, and all the office workers on the other floors had left for the day.

"They're not going anywhere," Neil announced.

"Good. Max, how are we on that transportation you promised?" Cal asked.

"I hope you don't mind, but I upped the ante. They're waiting outside, and well ... I'll leave the heavy lifting to you, Mr. Stokes."

Everyone was ready. Cal and Daniel would go in with Top and Gaucho. They were wearing street clothes, but now at least everyone was armed. Neil would stay at the apartment with Jonas, Dr. Higgins, Diane, Anna and Lydia until the hard part was over. Then it would be on to the airport for the whole crew.

Neil had insisted on going on the operation, saying he could monitor the situation from the laptop. By remaining close to them he could easily relay the intel they would need. However, Cal wanted him to stay put and that they'd stay in touch via the phone. Neil reluctantly agreed, but also felt relief: deep down he knew he wasn't up for going into battle this time. His nerves still rattled, and it would take more than a few hours for him to be back to one hundred percent.

He'd promised to keep Cal and the others informed. As he watched them leave, grim nods were exchanged while they stepped out the door.

* * *

MAX'S SURPRISE for the men turned out to be three gleaming black Lamborghinis, driven by three members of the French Intelligence Service. No names were exchanged, but when Cal slid into the passenger's seat of the little high-end car, it was obvious he had been paired with the leader of the three.

"You have weapons?" the man asked.

"We do," Cal said.

"Good, I want to know your plans when you get to these men you're paying a visit."

Cal knew what he *wanted* to do, but he didn't want to say that to the man driving. "Getting to the objective, we don't want anybody to get hurt, so we'll be as careful as we can," Cal answered.

"In my opinion, you should kill them all," the man said, taking Cal by surprise.

"I'm sorry. Why would we do that?" Cal asked.

"These men are known to us and to my government. They make many headaches. No one who matters in my country would care if you killed them."

Was this guy being serious with him? Cal really couldn't believe what he was hearing, but then to prove the point the man added, "We have been sent to clean up any mess you leave behind. The streets will be swept for witnesses. You and your friends will be taken to the airport after you have completed your mission."

"Well, Holy Mary, Mother of God."

The driver turned to Cal, grinned, and then made the sign of the cross. "Good hunting, my American friend."

* * *

MAURICE TRIED NOT to show his impatience. The Americans

had promised escalated bonuses should he find Rourke's information by certain time intervals. Now time was ticking away, and Maurice could feel dollar bills slipping through his hands.

Ian Rourke was tougher than he'd anticipated; he'd thought for sure that the twisting of the knife would have made the man talk. Yet, to the American's credit he just sat there bleeding, face pale, drenched in sweat, and smelling like he was halfway to his grave. But he *would not* talk.

Maurice knew that he was now walking a fine line. He would soon have to provide Rourke medical attention just to keep him alive. The leg wound was deep. Even though it had only been minutes, Maurice's access to the promised treasures would be completely lost to him if the knife's blade had hit an artery. Maurice's head snapped to the window at the sound of revving engines nearby. They were there one moment, then gone the next.

"What was that?" Maurice asked his men through the radio.

"Probably some Saudis racing the streets. There were three cars, but they're long gone now."

Those Middle-Easterners and their oil money, Maurice thought. Soon they would own his country, and Maurice would do anything he could to prevent that from happening. At this moment, he couldn't do anything about them, so he turned his attention back to Ian Rourke.

"Ian, we were once friends. Let's not let our relationship end this way. Come, tell me what I need to know, and you will be back in America before you can say Mickey Mouse." Maurice could see that Rourke was trying to form a reply. *Some smart comment, no doubt.*

Maurice opened his own mouth to warn him against it when the room went black around him. Maurice froze, waiting for the power to come back on. But then, instead of the familiar hum of generators, he heard the echo of gunfire from the other room, and he ran for the door.

* * *

NEIL HAD VECTORED them in perfectly. The drive-by had been the lead driver's idea. They roared by the office building at almost one hundred miles per hour, but they hadn't gone far and then they'd doubled back to the office building, slowly and quietly this time.

With Neil's assistance, they'd found a back way in, utilizing a service door where Daniel easily picked the lock, and then led the way into the building. The Frenchmen in the Lamborghinis remained in their cars, using high-tech thermal imaging to monitor the situation. Once they were tapped into the conversation, they augmented Neil's description of the building, providing live reporting on where the enemy was situated.

It was four men against six. Daniel grinned at the odds. It would be an unfair fight, given Maurice and his men thought they were safe. With the blanket of American approval, they believed they were untouchable. That was confirmed as the French Intelligence men relayed that there were no patrols, and that five men now sat in an empty office waiting room. Their weapons were not even at the ready.

When Daniel gave Neil the signal to cut the power, he and Cal rushed in first, catching the enemy completely by surprise. The men from The Jefferson Group did not hesitate.

* * *

IT WAS STUPID, he knew, but Cal waded into battle with a pistol in each hand. Daniel had given him a look before entering, questioning his judgment. But Cal had explained it to himself: *I don't want to have to reload on the fly.*

As it happened, that never became necessary. They moved in without a sound, the darkness hiding their movement. Daniel's first two shots took out the man straight ahead. The most immediate threat had already gone for his weapon, lying beside him. He never made it. The others weren't as slow and, through his peripheral vision, Cal saw more weapons being raised.

Rather than take one out at a time, Cal threw his hands out wide. He trusted in his aim, the hundreds of hours throwing lead down range creating muscle memory, and the fact was, he no longer had to look down the sight of a pistol. He pointed his body toward the target, and then bang, it was all over. It was different shooting with two weapons rather than just one. All his frustration, the thought of Liberty lying helpless in that hospital bed, the fact that the woman he loved had been in danger and the men around him had been threatened burst through his veins and sharpened his instincts.

Cal's shots did not miss their marks, and he hit two men center mass on either side of the room. One, two, three, four. Eight shots in total. The enemy was down. Four shots from Daniel, and then it was all over. Cal took a breath and tucked one of the pistols into his waistband.

"Clear," came the call from the French driver down on the street.

"Turn the lights back on," Cal said to Neil. The lights clicked on seconds later, and Cal saw there was one man in the room still alive. Actually, he was only halfway in the room, propped awkwardly against the doorjamb, his legs splayed out in front of him, blood seeping from multiple wounds. When Cal examined his face, he recognized it as the leader of the rogue band.

"It's Maurice," Daniel confirmed a split second later. Blood was seeping from the man's mouth, but Daniel still kicked his weapon away and searched him for any more. Then he moved on to the other room, allowing Cal to have a conversation with the Frenchman.

"Did you hurt Rourke?" Cal asked, tilting the man's head up so he could look him in the eye. The man mumbled something that must have been a French curse, probably calling Cal's mother a whore.

"He's in here!" Daniel called.

Cal tilted Maurice's head up again, remembering the promise he'd made to the man sitting behind the wheel of the Lamborghini. "There's some men outside who would like to speak with you. I'm sure they'll do a much better job of tearing you to pieces than I ever could."

They secured Maurice with a set of zip ties from the man's own pocket, and Cal and his team left the man there. Top and Gaucho towed along Ian Rourke as they made their way out of the building. A large SUV arrived just as they made their way outside, and the French Intelligence officer told them that it was their ride.

"We'll take care of the mess upstairs. These drivers have their instructions. They are to take you to the airport; there's a plane waiting. No one will stop you, but I would recommend leaving the city tonight."

"Don't worry, I'm more than ready to get home." Cal said to the man, shaking his hand.

More vehicles arrived and men in street clothes rushed into the building, setting to their grim task. They eased Rourke into the SUV. Gaucho pulled out a med kit and examined the wound on the former Bureau man's right leg. As soon as everybody was in the vehicle, the SUV sped away.

Cal had just turned in his seat to begin the interrogation, but Rourke asked first, "Is Anna safe?"

Daniel and Cal looked at each other. Cal could see the protectiveness cover a flash of anger in Daniel's eyes.

"She's fine," Cal answered, "but you're in for a long night."

Rourke grimaced as Gaucho pressed a wad of gauze into the man's wound. "Don't worry; I'll talk," he said, "You won't have to bring in Dr. Higgins."

Cal wondered at the extent of knowledge Ian Rourke had gathered about him and his team. They would find out soon enough.

"But it's not over," Rourke continued, "That's what I was going to tell you at the train station. I went there for Anna, but I had to tell you." The man was obviously struggling not to pass out, but he held on until he'd expelled his final words before slumping down in the seat. "It's the president. He's after the president."

CHAPTER THIRTY-NINE

Congressman McKnight hung up the phone and squeezed his eyes shut. The pain mounted behind his ear lobes. It was the beginning of a migraine for sure. Not only was he having to deal with repeated calls from the media demanding to know how he was going to close the huge gap between him and President Zimmer, but Republicans were beginning to whisper they'd made the wrong call and put the wrong candidate forward. The whispers intensified when speculation swirled around a landslide victory for the Democrats.

Public scrutiny and criticism were an everyday part of being a politician, and McKnight had made peace with that years ago. But this was the presidency, and he'd worked too long and too hard to lose now.

The doubts crept in, like vultures sneaking in to take a bite of a bloody corpse. They picked away without regard for his long fought plans. He had to believe that there still was hope. If he could just get the information he needed out of France and put it into the right hands here in America,

McKnight was sure that the tide would turn. If that were to occur, the election could sweep in the other direction.

The American people were sick of run-of-the-mill politicians. Even though Zimmer was the current popular choice, the winds of political change did not discriminate. Rourke had been promised dates, places, and even names. Even now as he thought about it, McKnight wanted to do a little dance. Instead of a dance, he strolled over to the side bar and poured himself a cold glass of water. He needed a clear head.

As he put the glass to his lips, the phone rang again. He almost ignored it until he realized it wasn't the phone by the bedside table. It was the phone in his pocket. He took it out and grinned. It was the Chairman of the RNC.

This is it, McKnight thought, his mood already rebounding.

"Senator," McKnight answered.

"Tony, are you alone?"

The Florida Congressman was so wrapped up in his anticipation that he missed the warning tones in the senator's voice.

"It's just you and me," McKnight said, sipping his water.

"I won't beat around the bush. It's bad news, Tony."

McKnight almost dropped the glass.

"Rourke's disappeared, and my go-between can't get hold of our French contact. I think we should prepare for the worst-case scenario."

"I don't understand! You told me this was a sure thing. Was it the French authorities? Have you had any word from them?"

"It wasn't the French, Tony. If it was, they're keeping a lid on things, more than I've ever seen them do before. As much as I hate to say it, because I'm the one who introduced you to him, I think Rourke was working with someone else. It's quite possible they took him. There's also a possibility Rourke had already made other enemies, but I think that is unlikely."

The senator's words sounded muffled now, like McKnight's head was under a pillow; he couldn't breathe.

"Tony? What do you want me to do? I feel like this is my fault."

"He didn't send anything back? Maybe there's a package coming in the mail?" McKnight hoped out loud.

"That's not how Rourke did business. You met him. He liked to do everything face-to-face. Listen, Tony. If there is something here that I should know about, maybe ..."

"No. Don't worry about it. I'll take care of it," McKnight said, even though he didn't really mean the words. They slipped out, just so he could get off the phone. For the briefest moment, he was tempted to tell the former senator: The Jefferson Group has ties to the president, and I planned to expose it all.

Having that information now felt like carrying a 500-pound log up the side of a boulder-strewn mountain. He needed help, and his body and mind willed him to ask for it. He shook the thought away. He'd never asked for help before, and he wouldn't start now.

"I'll call you back when I've amended my plan. Besides, I've got the debate tonight to think about. I'll see you there."

"I'll see you tonight, Tony. Good luck."

The call ended and McKnight dropped the phone to the floor. He imagined what his closest advisors would say. Unfortunately, some of them had already been saying that this was just his first shot, and that he could always come back and run for the presidency again.

But McKnight knew they were only empty words to placate him. In his mind, you only got one shot at the White

House. Not many people tried it twice and won. Of course, he could go back to Congress, and maybe he would find support to run for a Senate seat. But that wouldn't do. His ego wouldn't allow it; his dreams wouldn't allow it. There was only one thing he wanted, and if he couldn't have it, the world would be damned.

CHAPTER FORTY

It hadn't been quite as easy as driving straight to the airport. Maurice had missed Rourke's femoral artery. However, the wound was still bad enough they'd had to stop in order to stabilize him. That was before Rourke told them he needed to make one extra stop. Cal denied the request assuming it was some kind of trick.

Rourke continued to plead, telling them if they stopped, he would give Cal everything he needed, "I'll give you every shred of proof I have and more."

They stopped at a bakery, of all places. Daniel went to the door, as instructed by Rourke. He asked for the owner, who stepped out on the street. He took one look at the vehicle where Rourke had the window rolled down, nodded and went back inside. When he returned, he gave a slim package to Daniel, then went back to work in his bakery.

It wasn't until they were aboard the privately-owned CIA plane, once again courtesy of Andy, that the pain meds had kicked in and Rourke was in a frame of mind to tell them everything.

They'd listened with rapt attention when he told them

about his meeting with Congressman McKnight and about the surveillance he'd put in place over the previous months, first in Charlottesville, later in Paris, Amsterdam, and Vienna. He explained that it had been McKnight who'd given the order to shut it all down after Rourke got the information he so desperately wanted.

Cal was happy he'd asked the women, who now included Lydia, to wait in the private lounge in the back of the plane because then Rourke had shown them the files. There'd been more than enough proof in those documents to lock them all away for life.

They took a ten-minute break for Cal to confer with the others.

Dr. Higgins was the first to be asked the very important question: "Do you think he's telling the truth, Doc?"

"He hasn't given me any indication he's lying," Higgins answered. "I can't know for sure, of course, unless I use my normal protocol."

"I just want to know what your gut's telling you."

"Then I would say he's telling the truth."

Cal looked at Neil, "And, what do you think? Did he send this out? Is there anyway of proving that he didn't?"

"I've scanned his logs, and it appears he kept this information to himself. But like Doc said, it's impossible to tell. He could've erased certain messages or screwed with the time stamps. It'll take me a lot longer than thirty minutes to make a final determination."

Neither man provided the answer Cal was seeking; he wanted certainty.

"I don't think we should believe this guy," Cal muttered.

"I think we should," Daniel said. The conviction in his voice made everyone turn.

"Why?" asked Cal.

"Because of Anna."

"You think we should go on the word of someone I just met? Look, Daniel, I know how you feel about her. I know you guys share a history, but to base our next move on her intuition...? It's not how we do things."

Cal would've thought the comment might anger his friend. Sometimes a little heated debate was what they needed, but Daniel just looked at him with those knowing eyes. The Zen Master had already reached his conclusion.

"It's not what Anna said. Instead, it's what Rourke keeps saying about Anna. He wants to make sure she's okay. I think he went to the train station in order to save her life. He wanted to do the right thing."

Trent spoke up next. "Look, I haven't been with you guys since the beginning, but I'm with Daniel. Love will make you do some funny things, and I think this Rourke character is telling us the truth."

"Okay, let's say that he is," Cal said. "What do we do, then? Other than by his word, we can't tie it back to McKnight. And, as much as I'd like to, I can't walk up to him and shoot him in the head."

In the end, the group reached the consensus to get home as fast as possible to inform the president of all that had happened. He would make the call. Let the politicians pummel themselves into bloody heaps. After all, it was what they did best.

CHAPTER FORTY-ONE

"Mr. President, can we get you anything?"

"I'm fine. Thanks, Mike," Zimmer said to the host of the night's debate. "Would it be okay with your people if I took a stroll? I like to get the lay of the land before things get hot."

"Be my guest Mr. President. I'll be right here if you need me."

Zimmer nodded to the man, one of CNN's leading political pundits. He was fair, but Zimmer knew the anchor wanted the real scoop. Zimmer and McKnight needed to be differentiated, and the reporter from CNN wanted to be the one to cut that line tonight. If it happened, it happened, but the President had faith that he and McKnight would keep their promises to poke and jab about the economy, health care and the Middle East. There was nothing wrong with that. It was a debate after all. They would be honest with each other and with the American people.

"Harry, I want to take a walk up to the rafters. Do you think that will be a problem?" the president asked one of his secret service detail.

"No, sir, as long as you stay away from the railing. The place has been swept."

Zimmer enjoyed this part. He'd purposefully come early. He liked to walk through the aisles where constituents would soon be sitting, to measure the steps across the stage, to smell the air, and to feel the lights beaming down. When his schedule and the building allowed it, Zimmer most enjoyed climbing the stairs into the rafters. The lighting and stage hands practiced their craft up there and it was an old habit from the days he spent tagging along on the campaign trail with his father. Back then, Brandon would sit up in the rafters to watch as his father railed against injustice, promising voters he would do the honorable thing.

It had given the young Brandon Zimmer a unique perspective of politics. Not quite like God looking down from the heavens, but something akin to it. It was a view most Americans would never see.

As he climbed the wooden stairs, followed closely by his security detail, the past collided with the present. He felt the steps beneath him and the years fell away as he ascended. He was a kid again, exploring the inner workings of the theater, listening to the lighting crew describe how to obtain just the right angles and just the right colors to use in any given situation.

The president didn't have to say a word. His security detail knew the routine. They backed off to give him space, and let him soak in the feelings and bask in the memories.

He didn't insist on much, but he did insist on having this time whenever it fit into his schedule. He'd spent recent days worrying about Cal and The Jefferson Group. Luckily, former Marine Major B. "Andy" Andrews, now with the CIA, had managed to do the president the not-so-small favor of getting his friends back.

The group was in flight somewhere over the Atlantic;

everyone was safe, even Liberty was healing. And while Cal reported there was a tall tale to tell, the president was content the issue had been resolved. The culprit was in custody, and now he could focus on the election process. It was possible they'd even make it back in time for the post-debate celebration. They'd re-watch the debate. No doubt, Top and Gaucho would pick on him for some silly gaffe or misquoted fact. It was those moments when Zimmer felt normal again. He looked forward to it more than he thought possible. He'd missed his friends and the level of normalcy they brought to his life.

"Mr. President, you have a visitor."

"I'll be down in a minute."

"Sir, it's Congressman McKnight. He said he'd like to have a private word with you."

Zimmer took one last look over the railing and smiled. "Tell him I'll be right down."

"Well, sir, he came up here."

"Oh, all right." A moment later McKnight and the president were shaking hands. "Are you ready for this Tony?"

"Yes, Mr. President." The usual ease McKnight exhibited with the president wasn't there. Zimmer searched his face and figured it was probably just nerves. It was their first debate together. He decided to help McKnight.

"Look Tony, whatever happens tonight, I just want to thank you for running a clean campaign. I think we're making history here, and we should both be proud of that." All he got was a stiff nod from McKnight. "Did you make sure you hydrated today? I can remember my first debate. I was too busy all day and didn't have a drop of water. I got up there under the scorching lights and almost passed out."

McKnight still didn't respond. "Tony, is everything all right?"

* * *

McKnight stared at the president. How had he done it? For years, McKnight had secretly set up spiked obstacles, attempting to trap the president, and yet at every turn, Zimmer had somehow slipped away unscathed, somehow came out even stronger. Now the president was the overwhelming favorite to win the coming election.

Soon, McKnight would only be a footnote in history. If the Republican congressman lost in the biggest landslide victory of the twenty-first century, the media would have a field day.

The president's lips were moving, but Congressman McKnight heard nothing. He just felt the pounding in his head, the steady thud of his heart beating in his chest, and he heard the words of his father echoing in his ears. The drunk bastard would slap him from one side of the kitchen to the other screaming, "You'll never amount to anything! You're just a piece of shit! I don't know why we ever had you!"

He could smell his father's breath and suddenly felt the almost overwhelming and real fear that had crippled him as a child. Then, using his familiar coping mechanisms, he closed his eyes and cut off the visions. His father was dead. He was no small boy anymore. He'd held his own, and now he would do it again. No two-bit politician from Massachusetts was going to tell Antonio McKnight that the game was over. So, ever so carefully, he wriggled his wrists and felt the object settle in his palm. Then he cocked his head and rushed the president.

* * *

Zimmer didn't even have time to put his arms up in self-defense before McKnight crashed into him. The first thing he felt was the wood railing against his back. His mind told him that he was about to be thrown over the ledge, but then he felt the stabbing pain in his abdomen, followed by two more thrusts in rapid succession.

He looked over McKnight's shoulder to his unseen security detail. He tried to call out, but the words stuck in his throat. Then he saw shadows moving in the distance. On some level, he knew it was the Secret Service agents running to his aid, but they wouldn't make it in time. And then McKnight put his cheek against the president's and he whispered in his ear, "It was all me. I want you to remember that when you fall into Hell."

McKnight pulled away so that their bodies were no longer touching. The president didn't hear the shouts from behind the crazed attacker. He couldn't know that his agents hesitated to shoot because they were afraid of hitting him. Zimmer looked into McKnight's eyes and felt the hatred as keenly as if a red poker had been shoved into his eye socket. Only a few seconds passed, but to Zimmer it felt like an eternity.

Then for some reason, the images of his friends came to him. Cal. Daniel. Top. Gaucho. What would they do? As the four of them stood on the periphery of his vision, they whispered as one, "Fight back. Fight back."

The president could acutely feel the pain now, stabbing deep into his torso, but it was eclipsed by this new resolve. He reached out with his hands, grabbing McKnight by the belt, and Zimmer did the only thing he could think of. He focused on that tiny sliver of awareness that remained, and with an impossible strength born out of sheer necessity, he pivoted and heaved McKnight over the railing, and into the three-story chasm. He didn't hear the cries of alarm from below, the screams from the agents or the surprised inhale from McKnight.

The president slumped to his knees, his head resting on the middle railing, affording him a perfect view of McKnight's rag doll body splayed on the wood stage below. There were hands on the president now. He didn't feel them pull him to safety, but when they turned him over, Zimmer saw the descending fog, and it reminded him of a squall line tearing across the plains. Then it swallowed him completely. He closed his eyes and gratefully accepted the darkness.

EPILOGUE

F lags across the nation flew at half-staff. It was a time for mourning and a time to reflect on the senseless loss of life, a leader gone too soon.

Cal and Diane weaved their way through the streets without saying a word. The soft sounds of the Top 40 radio station weren't heard. There was nothing to say. They'd been too late. Diane tried to remind Cal that there was no way any of them could have predicted what had happened. There were still so many questions.

When they touched down in Charlottesville, they'd been greeted by the news. That had been three days before. The media was reporting the story that had been spun by the heads of the American government. Congressman Antonio McKnight had fallen to his death while rehearsing for the first presidential debate. In a completely unrelated event, the president had been struck down by an undetermined ailment.

Very few people knew the truth, and while Marge Haines had explained to Cal that it was better this way, Cal couldn't help but think Americans deserved to know the truth. Congressman McKnight was certainly not a hero and didn't deserve a single flag at half-staff. The man was evidence of all that was wrong with the political system. He had been crooked, conniving and evil.

As a show of good faith, and possibly as a step on his road to penance, Ian Rourke followed through on his promise to find out everything he could about Congressman McKnight. Rourke dug up his past, his business dealings, and even his sex life. Rourke's work was quick and efficient, and while certain pieces of McKnight's life were buried in the grave with the Florida politician, even Neil, who specialized in such things, was impressed that Rourke could make so many connections, so quickly. Much of it could never be proven in court, like the murder of McKnight's father which Rourke believed had come at the hands of young Tony McKnight himself. But it wasn't like the case was going to court.

Rourke explained to them that if anybody had been looking, the truth was there. But that was the key. Nobody had looked. The assumption had been that McKnight's character was of the highest quality. The president himself had brought him into his inner circle, trusting him enough to introduce him to his friends at The Jefferson Group. They'd all been duped.

As Cal drove past another group of mourners, he silently cursed the dead man.

When they finally arrived at their destination, the military cordon was on high alert. Steely-eyed soldiers watched over the meandering crowds from Bradley fighting vehicles and M1 tanks. Cal had never seen anything like it, and he wondered if they'd be able to get through. Even the fresh-faced soldier checking IDs looked like he would not allow the Queen of England to enter.

Cal parked the car in a reserved spot. He then opened the back door and lifted Liberty from the back seat. He set her on the ground gingerly, fastening a leash to her collar. The plan had been to leave her at the hotel, but ever since waking, Liberty had made it a habit to howl like a colicky baby every time Cal left the room. Even more than before, the dog was now Cal's constant companion.

Liberty looked up at him as if verifying his permission and support to walk. She would be sore for weeks, but the vet said it would be good for her to start getting some exercise to get the blood flowing again. She was on the mend, but for the time being, she remained wrapped in bandages that Cal had to check and replace twice a day.

The ID-checking soldier was just reaching out for Cal's identification when a voice from behind him called out.

"They're with me," Marge Haines said. As if to show she would tolerate no resistance, she repeated, "I said, they're with me." The tone told anyone in earshot that she was in charge. It wasn't rude, just exploding with authority.

The soldier gave Cal and Diane the once-over and then looked down at the dog. "My granddad had a German Short-hair. Good dogs." Then he looked up at his sergeant and tried to plaster a professional façade back on his face.

When they had moved past the military phalanx, Marge's face softened and she said, "It's good to see you, Diane." She touched Diane on the arm as they walked.

"Thanks for letting me tag along, Ms. Haines."

"Please, it's Marge." Then she turned to Cal. "Thanks for sending me that information by the way. We can't use it, but it was helpful convincing the Republican brass to go along with our story."

"How's that going?" Cal asked, making it obvious in his tone that he didn't agree with the spin that they were presenting to the American people.

Either Marge didn't recognize Cal's sarcasm, or she chose to ignore it.

"The election is postponed for the time being until both

parties can get together. That may take a couple of weeks to a month. But we don't want to see this thing go to the Supreme Court, and I don't think it will."

The question of what would happen with the presidential election was what everyone was talking about. News pieces were opened with the sorrow-filled eyes of a news anchor detailing the tragedy, but then quickly segued into the unprecedented consequences that would soon shape American history. In its centuries of existence, nothing like this had ever happened in an election year.

The only positive to arise from the situation was that both parties wanted an equitable solution. It probably had something to do with the loss of life and the somber attitude sweeping across the nation. It would have been an altogether different atmosphere had both candidates simply dropped out of the race. There were contingencies for that type of occurrence, but this? This was something new. As they followed behind their host, Cal knew that Marge Haines would have a strong hand in shaping what was to come. Her position in the White House, relationships in the legal world, and her force of character ensured that she would get her way. Of that, Cal had little doubt.

They had to pass through three more checkpoints before they got to the final door. There had been more than a few curious stares at the couple and their dog walking along the corridors. When they got to the room, Diane asked, "Are you sure I shouldn't just wait out here? I could take one of those seats and keep Liberty with me."

"No, it's okay, you should go with Cal," Marge said.

"You're not coming with us?" Cal asked.

"I've got a lot to do. I'll see you before you leave." With that Marge was off, already placing a phone call.

Cal motioned to the door. "Ladies first."

"I think you should go first, Cal."

Cal wouldn't admit this to anyone, but he didn't want to go inside. He didn't want to look Brandon in the eye. He didn't want to deal with the fact that he'd failed. Finally, he took a deep breath and stepped inside. Daniel was sitting on the windowsill and looked up when Cal entered. Cal gave him a nod that Daniel returned. Anna had left early that morning, back to running The Pension after a tearful goodbye with the Daniel. Cal hoped to see Anna again. She was good for Daniel, and the sniper deserved the best.

Cal's eyes drifted over to the hospital bed.

"Well it's about time you came to visit me," said the president. His voice was hoarse and his eyes sunken. Liberty pulled on the leash, and Cal gently pulled back. "Aww, come on, Cal. Let me say hello to the pretty girl."

Cal let go and Liberty rushed over to the president's bedside. Brandon reached down and stroked the dog's head. "See girl, now you and I look the same." The president patted his bandaged torso.

Cal knew he should say something, but the words just wouldn't come. Brandon must have read his mind because he filled the gap instead. "Diane, it's great to see you."

Diane walked up to the bed and offered her hand to the president.

"And here I thought we were friends. Don't I at least get a kiss on the cheek?" the president asked, with more than a hint of sarcasm.

Diane leaned down and kissed the president, who returned the favor. Diane moved back to Cal.

For a moment, there was an awkward silence, one Daniel didn't feel compelled to fill. Cal shot him a look, but Daniel ignored it. Once again Brandon waded in. "And how is everyone else? I hear Top is back in Amsterdam?"

Cal nodded. "He and Gaucho had to take Top's friend, Lydia, home. We just wanted to make sure she's safe. Rourke says his contractors are off the case, but Top wanted to make sure."

"Rourke is the security specialist that McKnight hired?" the president asked.

Cal nodded. "He's been helpful, which given the circumstances is a welcome surprise."

"And Neil and Doc Higgins?" the President asked.

Cal suspected that Daniel had probably told him everything, but Cal was grateful to be talking about other people and not the elephant in the room.

"Neil is rebuilding our network. It's not operational yet, but once you give us the go ahead we should be ready. Doc is back to overanalyzing our brain function."

The president nodded. "Daniel tells me that you're thinking about taking some time off."

It wasn't an accusation, just a question from one friend to another. Cal felt uncomfortable answering.

"Our last vacation wasn't exactly what I had promised Diane, so we thought we'd ... I mean, if it's okay with you."

"Of course it is," the president said quickly. "You all deserve it. You know that, and I've told you that many times. Besides, I'm going to be busy dealing with this," he motioned to his torso.

"About that..." Cal blurted, "I just want to say how—"

Brandon stopped him with a look, a look that said "*Don't keep going or I'm going to get out of this bed and slap the words out of your mouth. You know, the ways friends do.*"

"This," the president said, once again motioning to his bandaged upper body, "was not your fault. This was the act of a lunatic. If anything, you saved my life."

"Brandon, we weren't there. We should have told you. We were going to tell you but we just didn't get back in time."

"Will you please let me finish?" Zimmer said, rolling his

eyes and looking at Daniel as if to say, *"Don't you hate it when he does this?"*

"What I was going to say is if it weren't for those lessons you gave me, my body muscle memory never would have taken over and thrown that piece of shit over the railing."

For a moment, Cal didn't know what to say. Then Daniel chuckled, soon followed by Diane.

Cal saw that the President wore a broad smile, like the fact that he had just killed his political opponent didn't matter. That smile said everything was going to be okay, and maybe it would. Just like the president and Liberty, things would eventually get pieced back together.

Maybe they would be whole again. They all learned their lessons, but when Cal really thought about it, he realized what was most important were the people in that room. They were his closest friends, the ones that made him want to fight harder, to do the right thing.

When they all took seats on the edge of the president's bed, Cal's body relaxed. His mind turned onto a greener path, and as the president explained what would happen in the coming days, Cal grabbed Diane's hand, stole a glance at his best friend Daniel, and made a promise to himself that he would protect these three until the last breath left his body.

* * *

SENATOR WARREN FOWLER turned off the television and let out a contented sigh. The Chairman of the Republican National Committee had had a busy three days. The unexpected death of Congressman Antonio McKnight sent the entire election into a free fall, much like McKnight's experience.

Fowler was one of only a handful of people who knew the truth, that McKnight had gone off the deep end and attacked the president. Fowler had fully expected the White House to shut the Republican Party out, but they hadn't. They'd reached across the aisle and asked for assistance.

While on most days the men and women in the House and Senate wielded the most power, when it came to a national election, the RNC, DNC and its chairmen wielded the power to sway super delegates and electoral votes. Without the heads of the respective parties onboard, the election would be a contentious battle. Luckily, cooler heads prevailed, and that wasn't what was going to happen.

The Republican party would craft a plan with their Democratic counterparts. A couple of ambitious leading Republicans had whispered to the former senator from Wisconsin that they should fight for their spot in the White House, but Fowler had threatened them with their careers should a single one fall out of line.

Fowler knew the White House was lost for now. Zimmer would retain his seat in the most important house in the land. That didn't matter to the man who all of Washington believed had been pulled out of semi-retirement to lead a struggling Republican Party.

No, Senator Warren Fowler had what he needed. He hadn't known the specifics of McKnight's tasking to Rourke, of course, and Fowler would never again attempt to contact the specialist, but it didn't matter. Overhearing one of Rourke's conversations with McKnight had either been dumb luck or a gift from the heavens. Fowler didn't care which. What was important was that he had a name—a name that he'd long sought.

Senator Fowler opened the side drawer of his desk and pushed a well-hidden button in the back corner. The mechanism released the lid that held a secret compartment crafted into the bottom of the drawer.

Fowler extracted the metal framed picture and stroked

the glass pane. It was a picture of a small boy grinning at the camera, holding a football under his left arm. The boy had his entire life in front of him. He could have anything in the world, except his father.

Fowler had watched the boy over the years and tried to guide him from afar. He'd even used his influence when needed. Then the boy turned into a man and then into a soldier. When the soldier's Army career lay in ruins, Fowler stepped in as the brash soldier was about to be thrown in jail. All the while, the boy never knew of his father.

Senator Fowler knew his only son was born by a woman he had met at a campaign stop in Wyoming. She'd caught his eye on a trail ride, her skills infinitely better than his. He'd asked her to dinner, and she'd been so beautiful and understanding. They'd spent an adventurous weekend together hiking and making love.

He'd left and they promised to keep in touch. They both knew the relationship would never last, but they pretended it would.

One day she called to say she was pregnant. She thought he should know, and informed him that she didn't need anything.

He heard her, but he had supported both her and the baby anyway. She'd made him promise before she died to watch over their son. He'd made that promise willingly and with a whole heart. But in the end, he'd failed at his task.

Their son had died on some godforsaken snow-covered mountain. That was when Fowler had left the Senate. While he told his colleagues that he needed time and might never be back, he had spent his time away investigating and spending his money on men like Ian Rourke. There was a time when he believed he might never have the answer. But now he had it. He had a name—Cal Stokes.

Now he knew the name of the man who had murdered his

boy. Fowler knew that without a shadow of a doubt, and as he looked down at the picture of his young son, he stroked the frame one more time. Fowler said, "It's okay Nick. It'll all be over soon. Daddy's going to take care of you."

* * *

CLICK HERE TO GET STARTED ON THE NEXT BOOK IN THIS SERIES

I hope you enjoyed this story.
If you did, please take a moment to write a review HERE. Even the short ones help!

GET A FREE COPY OF THE CORPS JUSTICE PREQUEL SHORT STORY, *GOD-SPEED*, JUST FOR SUBSCRIBING AT CG-COOPER.COM

**More thanks to my Beta Readers:
Andrew, John, Melissa, Carl, Marsha, Wanda, Paul, Larry, Susan, Michael, Don, Glenda, Kim, Jim, Pam, Kathryn, CaryLory, Nancy, Julie, Bob, Phil, Craig, Alex, Marry and David. Thank you for being part of the family.**

ALSO BY C. G. COOPER

The Corps Justice Series In Order:

Back To War

Council Of Patriots

Prime Asset

Presidential Shift

National Burden

Lethal Misconduct

Moral Imperative

Disavowed

Chain Of Command

Papal Justice

The Zimmer Doctrine

Sabotage

Liberty Down

Sins Of The Father

Corps Justice Short Stories:

Chosen

God-Speed

Running

The Daniel Briggs Novels:

Adrift

Fallen

ABOUT THE AUTHOR

C. G. Cooper is the USA TODAY and AMAZON
BESTSELLING author of the CORPS JUSTICE novels
(including spinoffs), The Chronicles of Benjamin Dragon and
the Patriot Protocol series.

Cooper grew up in a Navy family and traveled from one
Naval base to another as he fed his love of books and a
fledgling desire to write.

Upon graduating from the University of Virginia with a
degree in Foreign Affairs, Cooper was commissioned in the

United States Marine Corps and went on to serve six years as an infantry officer. C. G. Cooper's final Marine duty station was in Nashville, Tennessee, where he fell in love with the laid-back lifestyle of Music City.

His first published novel, BACK TO WAR, came out of a need to link back to his time in the Marine Corps. That novel, written as a side project, spawned many follow-on novels, several exciting spinoffs, and catapulted Cooper's career.

Cooper lives just south of Nashville with his wife, three children, and their German shorthaired pointer, Liberty, who's become a popular character in the Corps Justice novels.

When he's not writing or hosting his podcast, Books In 30, Cooper spends time with his family, does his best to improve his golf handicap, and loves to shed light on the ongoing fight of everyday heroes.

Cooper loves hearing from readers and responds to every email personally.

To connect with C. G. Cooper visit
www.cg-cooper.com

65173245R00143

Made in the USA
Columbia, SC
13 July 2019